RAMPAGE

DEUCES WILD BOOK TWO

ELL LEIGH CLARKE

MICHAEL ANDERLE

L M B P N

DISRUPTIVE IMAGINATION

RAMPAGE TEAM

Thanks to the JIT Readers

John Ashmore
Mary Morris
Peter Manis
James Caplan
Kelly O'Donnell
Paul Westman
Larry Omans
Micky Cocker

If I've missed anyone, please let me know!

Editor
Lynne Stiegler

CHAPTER 1 NICKIE

Rebus Quadrant, Aboard the _Penitent Granddaughter_, Nickie's Quarters

The Skaines had a rather skewed idea of luxury. There were no bright colors. None of the furniture was comfortable, plus it was all so utilitarian. Nickie could appreciate that sort of aesthetic sometimes, but she was rather opposed to it when _her bed_ fell into that category. She was pretty sure the grey rectangle beneath her was made of concrete rather than anything that was supposed to be used to stuff mattresses.

She really should replace it eventually. And probably Grim's, though she wasn't actually sure if a species with entirely different physiology slept the same way humans did. She supposed she could add it to the shopping list the next time they were in port.

Despite the discomfort, she made no effort to get up. Instead, she stayed right where she was on the bed, legs akimbo and one arm splayed out to her side. With her other hand, she absentmindedly tossed a holoball toward the ceiling, catching it as it came back down and occasionally sending it floating around the room to watch its iridescent colors bounce off the walls.

When it came back into range she batted it abruptly, like a cat with a bone to pick. It careened around the room before coming to a halt above her again.

It wasn't quite as satisfying as actually getting to wail on someone. The little floating ball didn't fight back. In fact, it didn't react at all. It was a floating orb of light.

Meredith suggested, *I'm sure Grim or Durq would be happy to try to entertain you.*

A few minutes later, she added, *Or at the very least, they wouldn't mind if you made an appearance.*

Nickie heaved a sigh and sat up on the bed. She closed a hand around the holoball, and it vanished in a spray of glowing particles.

Look, it's not my fault if I just want to punch something every so often. And it's been ages since I was able to, at least in any worthwhile capacity.

She folded her arms over her chest after she made the argument.

Meredith replied, *Considering you have actively neglected to find any less violent coping mechanisms, I calculate that it is your fault, but that is neither here nor there.*

Nickie scowled, mouth twisting to the side, but Meredith plowed onward.

As I said, they would be fine entertaining you.

Nickie shot back, *They're both lousy at poker. Durq's a baby and basically announces what his cards are as soon as he has them, and Grim has the worst poker face ever.*

She made faces at the wall across from her as she grumbled, as if the wall had personally offended her.

Meredith offered, *You could play poker with me, if you're that hot for the game. It's not as if I'm going anywhere, and it would be slightly more practical than chomping at the bit for a fight all hours of the day and night.*

The suggestion only led to Nickie groaning and tumbling back down on her bed. It didn't do much to cushion the fall. "You're a *computer*," she blurted. "What sort of chance do I stand against you? Especially when I can't even hide my cards from you."

I wouldn't peek, Meredith assured her.

Nickie flung one forearm across her face.

No, just leave me here to wallow in my misery. I figure eventually I'll just die of sheer boredom, and then I don't need to worry about anything.

Meredith didn't respond to that, and for a moment the room was quiet. Nickie's holoball appeared in one of her hands again, and she passed it back and forth from one hand to the other for a minute.

Eyes tracking the ball, her tone was slightly distracted when she eventually asked aloud, "Has the time lock on the next entry in my aunt's diary opened yet?"

Not yet. As I said before, you don't need to ask. I will let you know as soon as the next entry unlocks. I'm not going to spontaneously go back on that decision and hold the entry hostage.

Nickie grumbled and folded her arms under her head, letting the holoball float aimlessly back and forth above her. Without any instruction from her, it lapsed into its default behavior, its colors gradually shifting as it drifted in geometric patterns. Hypnotically, almost.

Nickie shook off her stupor after a few minutes with a thoughtful hum. *Do you think I could train with one of your little minion bots? I mean, they had those tasers that one time. I could make it work.*

No, sorry. If my being a computer is considered cheating in poker, I'm quite certain it would also be cheating in combat. I know you have strong feelings about that.

Nickie sighed. *Oh, come on! I'm dying here! I'm going to shrivel up into nothing, and then what will you do? Pilot me around like a zombie mech? I'm pretty sure that would be a very short-term and smelly solution.*

Meredith said nothing more, no matter how long Nickie waited. Finally, Nickie stuck her tongue out and blew a raspberry at the ceiling. Whether it was a defiant or victorious gesture, even she wasn't entirely sure.

Rebus Quadrant, Aboard the *Penitent Granddaughter*, Bridge

"Nearly to Themis," Nickie observed, ignoring the remnants of lunch for the time being and focusing her attention on the main viewing screen. Someone else would clean up later. "Feels like it's been a lot longer than it actually has."

"A lot's happened," Grim agreed, tapping the end of a fork against an empty tray in no particular rhythm. "You're kind of the reason for it," he pointed out. "You shouldn't be surprised."

Nickie stuck her tongue out at him. "Molly helped. She's at least as good at wrecking shit as I am."

"That's not comforting," Grim drawled, setting the fork down and folding his arms. "Neither is the fact that we're swanning back in purely to give them deadly weapons they probably don't know how to handle." He shrugged. "But I guess some things can't be helped."

"I'll give them a crash course on how to not blow up their colony," Nickie assured him, her chin dipping in a brief nod. "To absolve us of any responsibility if they manage to blow up their colony."

Grim covered a laugh behind his hand before he could help it, his mandibles twitching wide open for a second before pulling tight to his face again. "Very comforting," he replied, putting as much sincerity behind the words as he could manage. He couldn't quite keep a straight face.

They lapsed into silence after that. Nickie picked at the last bits of her lunch and Grim let his thoughts wander. The bridge was quiet, save for Durq fussing at his console on the other side of the room.

"Do you suppose they've done all right for themselves?" Grim wondered as the little spit of rock that was Themis loomed closer on the main viewing screen. "I mean, we haven't been gone that long, and they seemed to have everything they would need." He hesitated. "But they also seemed a bit, uh…danger prone?" The last part came out sounding like a tentative question.

Nickie flicked a leftover crumb across the table at him. "How am I supposed to know?" she asked, one eyebrow rising. "We haven't exactly kept in touch with them. Or I haven't, at least. Meredith?" She looked toward the nearest speaker.

"I saw no reason to interrupt their daily activities," the EI replied. "Especially considering we were fairly occupied.

Regardless, I don't believe we've been gone long enough for any real trouble to find them."

Grim squinted suspiciously and Nickie half expected him to say "knock on wood," but she supposed that was a uniquely human superstition. Instead, Grim simply turned his attention back to the main viewing screen.

"We should have called." He sighed. "It seems like something's off."

"Should I make you a tinfoil hat?" Nickie asked dryly, propping her chin up in one hand. "I'm sure one of the bots could bring me some foil. I even know a bit of origami." She paused, eyes drifting up and to the side in thought. After a second, she mused, "Granted, you're already an alien, but I associate tinfoil hats with conspiracies."

Grim flicked the crumb back at her. "So are you—an alien—from my perspective," he pointed out. "And I'm not the one who keeps promising people 'Oh, sure, I'll go chasing after this dangerous target for you' for spurious reasons."

"I'm a vigilante," she insisted primly. "I help people, and look badass doing it." She brought a hand to her chest. "I am just upholding my role."

Your self-assigned role.

Hey, no one objected. You've gone along for the ride pretty easily so far, so you don't get to complain.

Dare I ask, but how exactly would I protest, even if I felt inclined to do so? We've already determined that piloting you like a zombie mech is out of the question.

I stopped paying attention once you confirmed you didn't feel inclined to protest. What was all that?

Nothing important, evidently.

Grim cleared his throat. "You know, it's obvious when you're having a conversation that no one else can hear."

The corners of Nickie's lips curled down in a delicately melodramatic pout. "It is not," she insisted. "I'm an amazing actor."

"You make faces," he continued as if she hadn't said anything. "It's a bit like watching someone rehearsing for an improv show."

Nickie blinked at him slowly. "How...the *fuck* does someone rehearse for an improv show?"

"Exactly," he answered earnestly.

Nickie snorted and tossed her fork at him, only for it to sail harmlessly past his shoulder and land on the floor. One of the cleaning bots—Brandy, the glimpse of copper plating confirmed—picked it up a second later and trundled out of the room with it like a dog with a bone.

"Breaking atmosphere in five minutes," Durq announced once it became apparent that neither Nickie nor Grim were paying attention. It was more of a mumble than a real announcement. He hunkered close to the console he was frequently seen at, largely because it was the only one big enough for him to bodily hide underneath in a pinch.

Nickie practically bounced up, rolling her shoulders and shifting on the balls of her feet for a few seconds. She gave her arms a shake afterward, satisfied that she was loosened up for anything that might happen.

Soon enough, there was the telltale rumble of the ship passing through the outer layers of the atmosphere and slowing, then the juddering bump that told them they were in the lower levels.

A few minutes later the ship touched down delicately on terra firma. "I'm attempting to hail the colony to let them know that we're landing, but I'm not getting any response," Meredith reported.

Nickie tensed, undoing her previous efforts to loosen up. "Any suspicious activity?"

"None that I'm picking up, but that in and of itself isn't comforting. I'm not picking up much of anything."

"What, it's just gone dark?" Nickie asked, incredulously before shaking her head sharply. "Just... Never mind, we'll figure it out once we get down there. You ready to go?" The last was directed at Grim as she turned to face him.

"As I'll ever be." He sighed and fell into step beside her as she strode toward the door that led out of the bridge.

Nickie paused once she got to the door, and pivoted on one foot. She pointed an imperious finger at Durq so suddenly that he recoiled slightly as if he thought she was going to scold him for something. She let her hand drop back to her side as she commanded, "You stay on the ship."

"As if that was ever in question," Grim muttered almost silently.

Durq's response was to duck under his console without complaint as Nickie and Grim left the bridge together. They always looked so badass, but dwelling on it wasn't going to do him any good.

As they left, Nickie couldn't help but recall Meredith's earlier words.

"Oh, I don't think we've been gone long enough for them to get into any trouble.' Buuuuullll shiiiiiit. Famous last words right there, Mere. You jinxed everything.

I have my doubts about a statement being the cause of the current dilemma, but if it makes you feel better, so be it.

They didn't say anything until they were off the ship and standing at the base of the ramp. Even just a cursory look around told them that it was deserted.

Grim cringed when Nickie cupped her hands around her mouth and hollered abruptly, "Anybody out here!?"

She stomped one foot and huffed like a discontented Clydesdale. "Wait here," she commanded without looking at Grim, already on the move toward the outpost. "At least until we know if it's safe or not."

"You don't need to tell *me* twice," Grim assured her as he took a seat on the airlock ramp. He watched Nickie's back as she got farther away. It wasn't until she disappeared into Tykis Outpost that Grim glanced over his shoulder. The idea was tempting, to just head right back up the ramp and into the ship. There were weapons on the ship, after all. He would probably be more useful if he had one.

But he was self-aware enough to know that if he went back onto the ship, he probably wouldn't come back off. He folded his arms nervously. After all, the crew—such as it was—didn't need *two* people hiding under their consoles every time a crisis hit.

Rebus Quadrant, Themis Colony

The main hall was quiet when Nickie stepped inside. She could hear the sounds of electronics buzzing, but there were no voices or sounds that heralded any sort of activity. Her footsteps echoed as she walked.

She slowed to a halt in the center of the main hall, arms tense at her sides. It felt like something was going to happen—like something was *supposed* to happen—but instead, everything just remained silent.

Remaining alert, Nickie plucked her trio of drones out of her belt pouch and tossed the metallic orbs into the air. They whizzed off in separate directions, and Nickie started walking in a fourth.

She paused at the mouth of a deserted hallway and waited. Then, slowly and cautiously, she drew her gun with one hand and her boot knife with the other. Only once she had a weapon in each hand did she begin the trek down the hallway, occasionally time-slicing her attention to the video feeds from her drones. They were having much the same luck as she was when it came to finding other people, which was none at all.

Any signs of...anything?

Not yet. I would have said something if I had anything relevant to offer.

Yeah, yeah. She looked behind her before moving forward again. *I know the drill. Can't say the nasty smell is making me think this is going to end well.*

There was a T at the end of the hallway, and Nickie peered down the left side first. She couldn't see anything in the half-light. It looked just as abandoned as the one she had just walked down.

Presumably the various doors along the hall were the same, or else there would have been *some* sign of someone being there.

I should tell you, the time lock on your aunt's diary has expired. The next entry is available for you to read.

Nickie couldn't help but huff out a laugh, shaking her head. "She always did have a theatrical sense of timing," she mused. "Surprisingly, I'll have to read it later. I'm up to my ass in mystery and danger here, and that's probably a little more important. But only a little."

She turned to look down the other side the hall, and just as she finished talking, she very nearly squealed in surprise as one of her boots slid out from under her like a rollerblade on a waxed floor. She landed on the floor, doing an impromptu split.

You didn't see that!

Of course not. That was perfectly normal.

Nickie glowered at thin air as she picked herself up, and

she looked down to see what she had stepped in. She froze when she saw what it was.

It was blood, spattered around the hall as if it had been sprayed in an arc all the way up one of the walls and onto the ceiling. Slowly, her eyes traced the trail on the floor back to a body slumped against the wall. The throat had been torn out so aggressively that Nickie could see the neckbones.

There were two more colonists slumped against the wall farther down, one with a hole through the chest and the other with a laser blast through the head. Even farther down the hall, there was one more body, looking thoroughly ravaged, as if it had been set upon by wild dogs.

No question about the smell, then.

A door at the end was open. Even from here she could see the flood of half-congealed blood that had flowed out into the hall. Instinctively she didn't want to see what was beyond the door, but she knew she had to look.

One by one, the drones began to find similar evidence, finding more and more bodies in the remotest sections of the outpost. It was as if the colonists had been trying to run, only to be chased deeper into the halls where they were massacred.

Nickie picked her way along the hall, stepping over bodies and around pools of blood. By the time she reached the open door, her grip on her gun and her knife were so tight that her fingers were starting to hurt.

She entered the room gun-first.

There was only a single body in the room. The throat had been torn out just as violently as the last one, but that wasn't the worst of it. The worst was the fact that it was hanging from the wall, nailed in place by a mining spike through the chest. It was like a banner to announce who had been there.

Between the laser injuries and the claw marks, Nickie knew *exactly* who had been there. She would always be able to recognize Skaine handiwork.

She backed out of the room, her nostrils flaring against the smell of blood and her breathing coming faster. She was angry enough that she wanted to rip the entire outpost down at that moment, but it wouldn't help her. She clamped her mouth shut and sucked in a deep breath through her nose, before breathing it out again—*in, two, three, out, two, three.*

Nickie.

Meredith interrupted her thoughts before they could go down even darker paths.

I've found records of a sealed fire door that is normally not supposed to be sealed. It's roughly twenty stories below-ground.

Nickie took another deep breath and sighed it out, loosening her hold on her weapons as she did.

Some of the colonists. They must have managed to flee into the mines.

She was already on the move, following the map that Meredith brought up on her HUD. She broke into a run after a few paces, and she reached the lift down into the mine in what felt like a few heartbeats.

Not that it actually meant much. The lift doors opened, but the lift was nowhere to be seen. She could see the lift cable, but when she stretched over and caught it, it swayed far too much for both ends to still be attached. She recalled her drones and put them back in her pouch.

Nickie backed up a pace and searched the area until she found a post long enough to brace the lift doors open, then caught the cable again, gripped it tightly in both hands, and jumped.

She dropped through the shaft like a stone, as if she weren't even holding the cable. She kicked her legs out so the soles of her boots met one wall, and she slammed her shoulder against the adjacent wall. She leaned into the corner, and she swore she could smell the soles of her boots starting to smoke as she tried to slow herself. Her jacket had to be in tatters.

When at last the cable snapped taut, Nickie had slowed herself down enough that she didn't wind up with a case of whiplash, even if she nearly bashed her head against the wall. Still braced into the corner like an awkward spider, she gave the cable a wary tug to make sure it wasn't going to try anymore funny business. When it remained tight, she began to shinny her way down the cable to the bottom.

It seemed like hours had passed before she saw a crooked, shapeless lump at the bottom. She cringed when she realized that the only thing it could be was the crashed lift. She let go of the cable and dropped the last several yards, landing on top of it with a metallic bang.

Think the Skaines cut the cable?

Most likely. We already know dirty tactics are not beyond them.

Nickie grunted but otherwise didn't reply.

There were half a dozen bodies still in the lift when Nickie pried the emergency hatch open and dropped in. She stepped over them carefully.

Surprisingly low fatality rate for a fall like that.

The observation felt cold and clinical as she made it.

In all likelihood, not all of the colonists came down at once. They would not have fit.

Somehow that only made it seem all the more depressing, and Nickie was quick to pry the lift doors open and step through.

The mines themselves weren't much better. There were emergency lights scattered every few yards through the larger tunnels, but the auxiliary shafts were pitch-black.

Nickie reached for her belt.

Switch the drones to audio mode, she told Meredith.

She made the decision and sent the three drones ahead of her, jogging carefully in their wake.

Meredith didn't reply, but Nickie could abruptly hear the creaks of the mineshaft settling ahead of her, and a grid suddenly blanketed her vision, shaping itself to the environment ahead of her. Even without any details, she at least had the rough shape of the landscape, and she would hear anything coming.

She didn't talk with Meredith on the way, focusing instead on keeping a steady pace with single-minded intent. Once her eyes adjusted she could just barely see the shine of her drones, and she followed them as closely as she could. They seemed to know where they were going.

At least until she was forced to grind to a halt when she realized the shaft ahead of her was blocked. From floor to ceiling, there was scarcely any space to pass.

"How would they have even gotten through here?" Nickie wondered aloud.

They likely got through before it was blocked. I suspect

weaker points throughout the tunnels were destabilized when the lift hit the ground.

Nickie hummed in acknowledgment and went to investigate the blockage. The rock and dirt and remnants of scaffolding groaned ominously as she ran a hand over them, and she backed up a pace.

While you can theoretically fit through the gap in the blockage, there is a high likelihood that you will be crushed trying to climb through when the debris shifts.

Not if I don't actually touch it.

Nickie backed up several yards, using the grid over her vision to line herself up before she burst into a sprint. At the last instant she leapt, hands stretched out in front of her. Straight as an arrow, she threw herself through the gap in the blockage, before arcing toward the ground. She landed hands-first and somersaulted, finally coming to a halt on all fours.

"I haven't been flattened," she observed after a few seconds, sounding slightly mystified by that fact. She levered herself to her feet and dusted herself off.

She didn't waste much time relishing in her victory, though. Her drones buzzed at one of her shoulders, so she waved them ahead and kept following them.

It seemed as if she jogged for half an eternity before anything changed, and she ground to a halt when she saw it at last.

There was a great dully-silver door ahead, battered and enormous. It looked big enough to hold up all of the mines on its own. It was only barely visible, the top and sides of it lit by flickering emergency lights. Nickie broke into a sprint as soon as she saw it, running halfway up a wall at one point to leap over a piece of abandoned mining equipment.

This door is typically unsealed, Meredith offered as confirmation once Nickie was standing in front of the door.

Shall I attempt to connect with Keen's communicator?

In answer, Nickie pulled her communicator out and stared at it expectantly. It clicked with static for a few seconds until, at last, "—llo? Is an— there? Th— Keen of— kis Outpost. Who— out there?"

So far underground, it was a miracle their communicators were working at all. Nickie clutched hers in both hands, knuckles going pale with the force of her hold.

"Keen? It's Nickie. Just hold tight. We're getting you all out of there."

Rebus Quadrant, Themis Colony

I can access the door control protocols, but I will still need you to manually fry the control box on the wall. Shall I let Grim know he'll need to bring you the necessary tools?

It took Nickie a moment to respond since she was staring at the massive door. Keen was saying something to her through her communicator, and he sounded shocked— too shocked to even be relieved or happy—but she couldn't make out most of the words through the static.

Nickie.

She jolted back to the present, spine straightening.

Yeah. Let him know. I'll...see if I can do anything while I wait.

She turned her attention back to her communicator and edged closer to the door. As she approached, the static cleared slightly. By the time she was nearly pressed flat to the door's almost-invisible seam, she could finally make out most of Keen's words.

"Nic—? Nickie, are—still there?"

The signal still wasn't perfect.

"Still here," she assured him. "Grim needs to bring me some equipment to open the door. How many of you are in there? And—" She took a breath, held it for a second, and let it out. "What happened?"

Keen was quiet for a moment. Nickie wasn't sure if it was because the signal weakened or not until he started speaking again.

"The Skaines ca— back," he answered, confirming what Nickie already suspected. "W—weren't ready. They ripped thr— outpost like tissue paper. I don't think th— happy about last time. S—pposed to be a secur—ty signal to open this— gain, but we haven't been ab— get it to connect."

Another gift from the Skaines, most likely.

He fell silent for a moment, and Nickie's grip on her communicator tightened. Finally, Keen admitted, "There aren'— ven a hundred in here. Maybe eighty-five."

Nickie stared straight ahead, eyes wide but unseeing as she tried to make that number compute.

Maybe eighty-five, but probably less.

Finally, voice flat and nearly robotic, she replied, "I need to focus on getting this door open." She terminated the call and put her communicator away.

Nickie cast around wildly, unsure just how sound-proofed the door was, then she spotted some long-abandoned scaffolding against the side of the corridor. She rounded upon it, then punched and kicked it. Venting her frustration, she didn't stop until it was only scrap metal.

She stood panting heavily through her teeth, looking back at the metal door she couldn't get through.

There wasn't much else she could do but wait for the tools she needed.

Grim eventually loped up behind her with a toolkit in hand. It had taken time, but much less than Nickie had expected it to. She whirled to face him when she heard him approach, and as she stared at him dully, he brandished the kit.

She grabbed it from him. "How did you get through so fast?" she asked, rifling through the kit for the tools she needed.

"Meredith told me about the obstacle course," he answered. "So I brought backup." He jerked a thumb over his shoulder to point behind him. When Nickie peered around him, she could see two of the house bots clustered around a jackhammer. And when she actually took a good look at him, it was apparent he was wearing a climbing harness and a backpack.

"Huh."

Nickie shook her head briefly to get her attention back on the current crisis. Tools in hand, she turned toward the door controls and set to work prying the casing open and snipping the appropriate wires once its innards had been bared.

Grim jumped back in surprise when the control panel sparked. The door shuddered, split, and stiffly began to slide open.

The bunker smelled once the doors were open, but

nowhere near as bad as Nickie had expected. Of course, that wasn't really surprising, in retrospect. It had been designed to hold the entire population of the colony in an emergency. There were so few of them that they'd had enough space to partition off a corner to use as a bathroom, and they still weren't cramped.

They looked haggard, like a breeze might blow them over or send them into a panic. They stared, bewildered, at the open doorway like they weren't sure what they were supposed to do.

Then Keen emerged, pushing his way past everyone else with Adelaide and Raynard on his heels.

Nickie knew she should say something to him, but he looked like a man whose world had fallen apart at his feet. Adelaide and Raynard looked haunted in a manner that Nickie knew would never go away.

She could feel her control on her temper fraying, so she turned on her heel, putting her back to the bunker before that could happen.

"I'll take the lead to make sure there's nothing in the mines," she told Grim, and she motioned for her drones. They started orbiting him like moons. "You hang back with the colonists. Make sure all of them make it out of the bunker, and none of them fall behind. They'll let me know if there's a crisis." She flapped a hand at one of the drones as it circled past.

"Okay, but— Nickie!"

Without giving Grim time to say anything, Nickie sprinted back into the mines, leaving him to shout after her ineffectually.

Nickie kept running with a single-minded focus. It

wasn't until she was passing what was left of the blockage that Meredith finally broke the uneasy silence.

Are you all right?

Nickie ground to a halt, going from sprinting to standing still so abruptly that she nearly gave herself whiplash.

Fine.

Nickie.

The Skaines came back. They did all this because of what I did last time.

She whirled, slamming one fist into what remained of the blockage. It trembled and creaked, and a few stones and clods of dirt tumbled down to the ground. She broke back into a run, but Meredith didn't let the topic drop.

Would you have preferred to have left them to their fate? You know what the Skaines had planned for them.

Nickie snorted, scoffing as she ran.

How does that suddenly mean this isn't my fault?

When Nickie emerged from the mines and returned to the airfield, Bradley and Lefty were unloading the weapons from the *Granddaughter's* cargo hold. If she squinted, she could see Durq cautiously peering out of the hold, mostly hidden behind the corner of the opening as the bots trundled up and down the gangplank.

She watched them quietly for a moment, standing framed in the entrance to the main shaft. Still watching them, she started to make her way back toward the ship, her mind still processing what she'd seen. What the colonists had been through. How those poor souls had died.

She felt nauseated as she walked.

When she arrived at the ship, she sat down on the gangplank and then toppled over backward, folding an arm under her head at the last second to cushion her landing.

Durq leaned slightly farther out of his hiding spot. It looked like he wanted to say something. Nickie wasn't sure what her face was doing just then, but he took one look at her expression and very visibly changed his mind. He shrank back into his hiding spot for a moment before scurrying back onto the ship entirely.

Slowly, Nickie sat up again, watching as the two bots worked. She supposed she could have gotten up to help them, but it wasn't as if they could get overworked. Instead, she stayed where she was, seated on the side of the gangplank. Eventually, she swung her legs over the side and dangled them toward the ground.

She tensed when Brandy and Lucky emerged from the mine alone, but a quick glance at the drones' footage showed that Grim and the colonists were still in the tunnels. Bots didn't need to worry about pacing or getting tired, after all.

Brandy and Lucky joined the other two bots, but she still didn't join in. She wasn't tired. Not quite, at least. She had been through days that had seemed eight times as long. Other than a tricky jump, she hadn't even done much that day, at least compared to previous events.

She wasn't tired, but she felt drained. Like she weighed a thousand pounds, each pound pulling her down toward the ground.

She looked up slowly when the first of the colonists came out of the shaft. Knowing that she would be alerted if anything went wrong, she hauled herself to her feet and made her way up the gangplank and onto the ship before any of them could spot her.

Considering everything she had caused and how she had practically run away from them earlier, she didn't quite want to speak with any of them yet.

As Nickie disappeared deeper into the ship the colonists kept trickling out of the mine, slow and befuddled like a horde of benign zombies. Grim was the last to step out, just a few paces behind Keen. The two of them kept everyone moving.

No one quite knew what they were supposed to do just then, so they did the only thing they really could. Those that were able—those who hadn't been too badly injured in the attack or addled by the stay underground—shuffled over to where the bots were depositing the weapons. They took a moment to peer at them, deciding what they were and where they were supposed to go before they began picking them up and moving them off of the airfield.

No one said it, but the idea loomed over them all the same; if another Skaine ship showed up on the horizon, none of them wanted to have weaponry just sitting out in the open, ripe for the taking.

Grim watched from just outside the mouth of the main shaft for a few minutes, eyes searching the entirety of the airfield before he decided that Nickie wasn't there. Finally, he pulled his communicator out.

"Meredith? Did Nickie make it out of the mines?"

"She's fine," the EI assured him. "She's back on the ship.

She needs a moment. Her involvement in this has her rather unsettled."

"Right. Thanks."

Knowing Meredith didn't expect or need a proper sign-off, Grim ended the call. He watched the ship for a moment before he sighed out a slow breath, put his communicator away, and jogged off to see how he could help the colonists.

CHAPTER 3 NICKIE

As half of what remained of the colonists decided what to do with the weapons, the other half of them slowly made their way back inside. Some of them were injured, and others were just too mentally and emotionally spent to do anything else. A few were simply making sure nothing went wrong. The injured leaned on the able-bodied all the way back into the main hall.

With Keen still out on the airfield, Adelaide and Raynard were the main escorts back into the outpost.

Reluctantly, Raynard shuffled into the center of the foyer to address the group. "Do we have any volunteers among the uninjured to help clean up?" he asked. He didn't need to specify what they were cleaning up. It was clear from the pinched expression on his face and the tight quiver to his voice that he meant the bodies of their friends and family members that had been left in the corridors.

"If you would prefer to stay here or head back out to the airfield, we understand," Adelaide added. "This...isn't the sort of thing we would force anyone to do."

After some mumbling and shuffling about, they wound up with ten volunteers.

It wasn't until they all split off into different hallways that Adelaide finally covered her face with both hands and bent over double. Her breath shuddered out irregularly as she fought the urge to start crying that had been sitting in her chest ever since the Skaines had returned. It took several moments, but she gradually managed to get her breathing back under control. Finally, she steeled her spine and straightened back up, closing her hands into fists at her sides to get them to stop shaking.

Raynard looped an arm around her shoulders, gave her a comforting squeeze, and pressed a kiss to the side of her head before they both started walking.

Although they both gasped in horror when they came upon the first scene of carnage and Adelaide couldn't quite stop an agonized sob from ripping out of her chest, they didn't let it stop them as they started taking down names and lining up bodies.

It wasn't until they came to a certain closet that they wavered. Raynard stepped in first and froze when he saw the grisly sight in front of him. He cast about for a moment, grabbed the first bin he saw, and evacuated the contents of his stomach into it.

Concerned, Adelaide went to follow him into the closet. Watching her shadow, Raynard bit out raggedly, "Don't." He extended his arm to stop her.

He spat into the bin and stumbled back from it, eyes on the cleanest wall. "Trust me, just—stay out there."

But none of them could afford to bury their heads in the sand. After only a few minutes to catch his breath and steel his nerves, Raynard turned toward the gory display, set his shoulders grimly, and wrapped his hands around the mining spike to heave it out of the wall.

Rebus Quadrant, Aboard the *Penitent Granddaughter*, Nickie's Quarters

Nickie's quarters weren't especially big. She hadn't really minded in the past, but it became very apparent that they were pretty small when she was pacing back and forth. She could really only get in a few good strides before she had to turn and go the other way.

Maybe she could knock out a wall and take over the quarters next door. It wasn't like she had to worry about taking someone else's room; only three of the cabins were occupied.

She was doing a very bad job of keeping herself distracted if she was thinking about redecorating. With a long groan, she fell back onto her bed, arms splayed out to her sides and her feet on the floor as she stared at the ceiling.

Meredith—

I've already told you, if I find anything unexpected on any of the outpost's security feeds, I will let you know.

Nickie groaned again and lifted a hand to drag it down her face, then flung it toward the ceiling. Her holoball appeared, and she twirled it in a circle, watching the lights shift. It did nothing to distract her, and after a moment it vanished. She let her arm fall back to the bed.

She knew what she wanted to do, but it felt too much like trying to reward herself for a horrible situation.

She thought about what Grim would say to her if he

knew what direction her thoughts were spiraling in. He would probably smack her upside the head and tell her to stop being ridiculous. It seemed like a very Grim thing to do.

She took a breath and heaved it out in a deep, blustering sigh, then sat up so she could lean back against the wall behind the bed. With a determined set to her jaw, she shoved her conflicted feelings into a box for the time being.

All right, Meredith. Let's see that diary entry. I might as well keep myself busy.

Of course.

The text appeared in Nickie's vision a moment later.

"Ninety-seven years ago now..." she mused with a low, impressed whistle. "I bet she hasn't slowed down at all since then." She couldn't help but grin as she decided, "I'll keep kicking ass for at *least* another two hundred. Can't let her upstage me."

With a contented sigh she settled in to start reading, drawing her knees toward her chest and folding her arms on top of them. She rested her chin on top of her arms as she got comfortable.

Planet Flex

Tabitha's footsteps were almost entirely silent as she made her way across the roof. To anyone without augmented hearing, they *were* entirely silent. Her coat caught the wind and revealed tight black pants and a fitted black top with a deep V-neck.

She looked down at her chest as she walked and smiled smugly.

Ryu came to her side, so quietly that even *her* hearing hadn't detected him. Tabitha hopped, then looked down again.

"Oooh, that was a good bounce."

"What are you doing?" Ryu asked, skeptically eyeing her.

"I'm *Rangering.*"

He blinked at her, eyes narrowing. "And what is that? Is there some aspect of this job I am not aware of? Does Barnabas do similar things?"

Tabitha was *very* much enjoying the way she swayed as

she swaggered across the roof. With her coat blowing back, anyone who was watching could see an absolutely curvy body in these clothes. The fact that no one *was* watching—that was the point of going across the roof at night silently, of course—didn't mean she couldn't feel good about how she looked.

As important as it was to look good, the mental image of Barnabas crossing this same roof with that swagger was just too much. Tabitha clapped a hand over her mouth to keep from snickering loudly and slammed a fist into her thigh as her whole body shook with laughter.

"Oh, my God." She gasped.

Ryu put his hands on his hips. "He does not. When Barnabas goes somewhere, he just *goes*. He doesn't worry about how he looks—"

"Stop, stop!" Her ribs were going to break if she kept laughing like this, but it was just too good not to.

Ryu rolled his eyes. "Kemosabe, *pay attention!*"

"I am *trying* to pay attention!" Tabitha wheezed. "You asked if Barnabas walks like this. Now I can't help but picture Barnabas in these pants."

Ryu stopped talking. He looked horrified, as if he knew what was coming and didn't want to hear any of it.

"Swaying his hips," Tabitha squeaked. She was trying not to laugh so loudly that the people in the buildings below could hear them, but she was having real trouble with that. "In *high-heeled* boots."

"Kemosabe, please don't." Ryu sounded panicked, his eyes looking everywhere trying to figure out a way to fix this problem.

"Coat blowing back in the wind to show his ass..."

There were tears of laughter streaming down Tabitha's face, and her chest felt like it was going to burst.

"I don't want to hear this." Ryu had sunk his face into his hands.

"*IN A V-NECK!*" Tabitha finished. She doubled over. "Oh, God, it hurts. It hurts so much. *Oh God, please make the pain stop!*"

"Now you are destroying my will to live," Ryu snapped, annoyed, "shall we get back to—"

She looked up at him, asking with an entirely too straight a face to go with the glint of humor in her eyes, "Do you think his tits bounce like mine?"

"OH, MY *GOD*." The vampire hissed like he was going to hurl. "Centuries," he muttered as he surveyed the rooftops. "I spent centuries fighting with honor, upholding and protecting the things I loved. I swore myself to an Empress without equal. I serve one of her highest generals." He glared at Tabitha. "And I am repaid with Barnabas and breasts."

"*Those* centuries weren't any fun," Tabitha told him confidently. She straightened and loosed the remaining few giggles, then wiped her eyes. "Ah, that was wonderful. I'll have to tell Barnabas about it the next time I see him."

"Please give me advance warning so I can be anywhere but where you two are talking." Ryu had an idea how Barnabas would respond to the image of him sashaying across a roof in tight leather pants. The only thing Ryu wasn't sure of was whether Ranger One's response would include nukes or just his lips pressed in a firm line.

"Oh, no." Tabitha smirked and slinked back across the roof. She swayed her hips and her shoulders as she walked.

His voice floated on the wind behind her, silent. "What are you doing? *Why* are you walking that way?"

"It's called 'sex appeal,' Ryu."

"Are you *sure*?"

Tabitha turned and glared at him. "You want to do five hundred push-ups right now? Because you're going to if you keep sassing me."

"I do not 'sass.'" Ryu scanned the alien city again with an expression of deep sadness. "Centuries," he repeated. "*Centuries.*"

"Yeah, yeah, keep being all—" Tabitha waved a hand at him. "Anyway, you have to be there when I tell Barnabas because it was your idea."

"It was *not* my idea!" The last thing Ryu wanted was for Barnabas to hear that *Ryu* had devised that mental image.

He would be so dead.

And then Hirotoshi would kill him again when he heard the story.

"You did, though," Tabitha argued. "You said, and I quote, '*Does Barnabas walk like that?*'"

"*No!* No. I said, 'Is there some aspect of the job I am not aware of? Does Barnabas do similar things?' That is *entirely* different."

"You meant, does Barnabas show off his ass like I do? Which he doesn't, because his isn't as nice as mine."

"They are two completely different... You know I simply wondered, does he let meaningless things distract him from his duty? I think you and I both know he does not."

"He and his friends spend *hours* trying to find new ways to cheat at chess," Tabitha stated in a tone of deep disgust.

"If that's not meaningless, I don't know what is. Anyway, you definitely asked while I—"

Ryu sighed, then questioned why he was about to say what he was going to say. The result was a foregone conclusion. However, he needed to try. His voice was urgent, a whisper. "Watch where you're *stepping*, Kemosabe!"

"Don't interrupt me!" she hissed back. "You asked while I was being all sexy, so any reasonable person would think that was what you meant."

Ryu rolled his eyes. He knew he wasn't going to persuade Tabitha on this score. When she had an idea, she could argue about it *forever*.

"Please *do* watch where you're stepping, though," he tried a second time.

The roofs in this city appeared to have been built by a madman. They overlapped and dropped off sharply, sometimes so ornate that one building would completely overshadow another. There were little carved statues everywhere, which were of course completely invisible from any street view of the buildings, and the slant was difficult even for ankles that were perfectly engineered.

Tabitha waved a hand airily. She strutted along a tiny ornamental fence as if it were a catwalk.

"Also, may I remind you that the Flexxent are multigender?"

"The Flexxent?" Tabitha looked at him with a confused frown.

"Yes, the Flexxent. The people who run this planet. Did you read *any* of the information Achronyx printed for you?"

Ranger Tabitha never reads my reports, Achronyx interjected mournfully.

"I read!" Tabitha asserted. "You just go on and on with all those..." She waved a hand again.

"Facts?" Ryu finished delicately.

Tabitha lifted her nose in the air. "I don't have to stand here and take this. Anyway, so what if they are multigender?" She frowned. "Wait, does that mean it's easy for them to have sex with themselves? Because if so, I just want to say I'm jealous."

Ryu gave her another horrified look.

Why had he volunteered for this mission again? Hirotoshi had just assumed he would go, and then Ryu had gotten some harebrained idea and said *he* should go instead.

Right now, he was having trouble remembering why.

Oh, right. He'd said that Hirotoshi got to have all the fun. If this was what Hirotoshi had been putting up with, Ryu was sorry he'd volunteered. Then he remembered the other man's small smile and his eyes narrowed.

Hirotoshi had known *just* what Ryu was getting himself into, and he'd let him do it.

Bastard.

"Ryu, does it mean they can just have sex with themselves? Like—" Tabitha made a gesture that was both confusing and far, *far* too easily understood.

"No." Ryu's head hurt. "No, it means they have multiple genders, not necessarily that they have sex with themselves."

"Not *necessarily?*"

"I mean, it's technically possible, but I really don't think—"

"Oh, I bet they do. They *totally* do. Achronyx, back me up."

I'd prefer not to get involved in this one.

"Useless," Tabitha muttered. She stalked ahead, throwing insults over her shoulder at Ryu, Achronyx, the Flexxent, and just for good measure, Barnabas. She bet Barnabas'd had something to do with this. He was stuffy. Achronyx was stuffy.

It all fit.

Ryu followed her as her whispers trailed off. The next time he looked up, she had disappeared.

"Kemosabe?" he whispered, looking around. Had she left to start the mission without him? *Shit.*

Worse, had she run off to ask a Flexxent if they ever had sex with themselves?

To his relief, he caught the sound of her annoyed voice filtering up from—

The ground.

Ryu jumped while pulling a switch on his harness. He drifted to the ground as an annoyed, "Sonofa*bitch!*" echoed through the alley. He arrived to find Tabitha lounging elegantly in a pile of garbage.

Or, at least, as elegantly as possible amidst food scraps and unidentifiable goo.

"Are you going to get up?" he asked doubtfully.

"I just set my leg." She inspected her nails. "It's healing."

"You fell off the roof."

She didn't look at him. "I don't want to talk about it."

"Because you weren't watching where you were going."

"You aren't listening."

Ryu looked up, "That's at least three floors."

"I'll have you know," Tabitha declared haughtily, pointing up, "that I did a fantastic 3 1/4 reverse non-tucked flip."

One eye raised, he asked. "You landed on the leg wrong?"

As if pried from her lips, Tabitha finally spit out "Yes!"

Ryu waited a moment before asking the inevitable. "Why *couldn't* you just say that?"

"Because a girl has to remain a little mysterious." Tabitha stood up and hobbled toward the mouth of the alley. "And none of this would have happened if you hadn't distracted me by talking about aliens screwing themselves."

"I didn't talk about that!"

"You brought it up." She looked up and down the street. "Achronyx, is it that way?"

Yes, Ranger Tabitha, but I feel I should tell you that—

"Excellent."

Ranger Tabitha—

"Not now, Achronyx."

You really should—

"Shut up, Achronyx." Tabitha hobbled slightly for a few more steps, then shook her shoulders out and started back into her catwalk strut. "Much better. That hurt like a bitch. Now that we're down here, shall we go with Option Two?"

"What's Option Two?" Ryu asked her.

"The front door."

Yud Skrow Lounge, City of Karkat

Two large aliens with flat-topped heads and what

looked to be either extremely complicated ears or multiple sets of ears were posted at the entrance to the building.

Tabitha sauntered to the door, nose lifted as she reached for the handle. The large aliens, however, closed ranks and glared down at her. One of them barked something in a gravelly voice, and the other pointed at a sign on the wall. It was white with black lettering, illuminated by a series of flashing lights in bright colors.

"They apparently want people to read that," Ryu remarked.

"I wonder what it says?" Tabitha squinted at it. "Nope, no clue." She shook her head. "Going in."

The aliens clearly had other ideas. They scowled even more fiercely as Tabitha tried to push her way past them. One of them snapped at her again.

"I can't read that!" Tabitha shot back.

They stood their ground, and one of them said something to the other, still speaking their own language.

"Ohhhh, they think they're so tough. They think we can't get in." Tabitha stomped away from the entrance with Ryu close behind. "Just because they can read a language we don't. Well, I know languages *they* don't know." She looked back at the aliens and jerked her chin. "*Anda a la concha de tus madres y chupas pija.*"

"Do I want to know?" Ryu asked.

"Not worth it." She shrugged. "People in Buenos Aires didn't swear as well as Bethany Anne. Just the classics, really. I don't know how to tell someone to take a moose dick in the ear in Spanish. It's 'moose' that's tripping me up."

"Uh-huh. And how are we planning to get into the

building? You know, while we're here." Did Hirotoshi have to herd her around this much, Ryu wondered. He'd have to ask when he got back.

Tabitha sighed. "I guess we're going to have to play alien knock-knock."

"I hate alien knock-knock." Ryu sighed. "Let's play something else."

"Like what? Some…Japanese…" She waved her hands in his general direction. "How did *you* get into places people didn't want you to go?"

"Generally, I didn't. Or, if I did, it was in a battle, and I went in through the front door with a battering ram or a mounted charge."

"What was it like living such a boring life? I would *not* have lasted there."

"No, you would not. For many reasons. A young woman who made a career of sneaking into people's… You know, I'm not sure how to compare what you've done and what you could have done in my youth. Sneaking into people's treasuries or listening to their secrets, I suppose."

"Uh-huh." Tabitha crossed her arms. "So what's *your* idea, if you don't want to play alien knock-knock?"

Ryu approached the aliens and bowed respectfully. "A pleasant evening to you," he said. "My associate and I wish to partake of your…"

"Drinks," Tabitha finished. "We want to have some drinks."

The aliens stared at them impassively.

Tabitha snapped, "So what do I have to do to get in, dickhead?"

The alien only stared at her.

"By the way, are these Flexxent?" she asked Ryu.

Ryu narrowed his eyes. "Perhaps? I have no idea."

They are, Achronyx said. *And Ranger Tabitha—*

"Not *now*, Achronyx." Tabitha studied the two aliens. "I don't think I want to ask about whether they have sex with themselves."

"You'll probably piss them off."

"Well, they've pissed *me* off!" She frowned. "They aren't just letting us in, and they won't even talk to us." She snapped her fingers. "Here's the plan. The one on the left— I rip his head off and beat his buddy to death with it. Then I rip *his* head off, too, and we go in and use them as bowling balls to knock people over. Those heads are huge. It could work."

"I think we should have a Plan B."

"You *would* say that. You've been no fun this whole night. 'Watch where you're going.' 'We should have a Plan B.' Who are you, Hirotoshi in a Ryu mask?"

Ryu bowed. "That is a fine compliment."

She shook her head. "No, it means you've got a stick up your ass."

"Hey," one of the aliens said in Torcellan. "Either leave or stop being rude and speak something we understand."

Tabitha stopped. She turned around, and her eyes began to flash red.

"I'd be happy to," she told the alien sweetly. "Do you understand the language of *Violence?*"

City of Karkat, Planet Flex

The patrons of the Yud Skrow Lounge were some of the richest in Karkat. They sat at tables carved of pure crystal and dined on a parade of complicated dishes, typically numbering thirty-five or forty per meal. The waiters wore black, and never spoke. The patrons conversed in low voices, so as not to be heard over the sound of the seven captive Hafe Fish trilling in perfect harmony from their tank.

There were no reservations, and the guest list was set for months in advance, the guests carefully curated and seated to ensure no violent rivalries surfaced in such a refined atmosphere.

When the door shuddered on its hinges, therefore, it was a surprise to every one of the aliens in the lounge.

Several screamed and fainted. The Hafe Fish shrieked and fled to the corner of their tank in a cloud of purple ink. At a table concealed in the shadows above the lounge floor, a Flexxent in an elegant suit raised a single finger for his guards.

Though the guards stood at the ready, they wouldn't advance through the lounge without their employer's approval. Guards in armor with guns hardly complemented the atmosphere Benet Aljun'ra wanted to cultivate.

The door shuddered again, and this time there was a scream from outside. Waiters, terrified of whatever was outside but even more terrified of Benet's anger, ushered the guests out the back exits as the door shuddered on its hinges three more times in close succession.

Finally, with a crash of splintering wood the door blew inwards, broken in two. One of the bouncers was thrown headfirst through the open doorway briefly, pulled back, and then thrown through the door to sprawl on the ground, toppling several crystal tables.

"Finally." A woman dressed in black threw the second bouncer in as well and sauntered through the doorway, brushing her hands. "I have to hand it to you, Ryu, that was a good idea."

"I in *no way* suggested using the guards as a battering ram." The voice sounded both bored and annoyed.

She looked over her shoulder and rolled her eyes. "Yes, but you did *mention* battering rams. I'm trying to give you credit as an integral part of this mission. Why can't you take a compliment?"

In the shadows, Benet Aljun'ra gestured again with one finger.

Two guards fired, and both bullets hit the woman square in the chest. She went flying back through the doorway, and Aljun'ra smiled when they heard her voice from the street.

"You bastard!" she bitched. "That hurt my ta-tas!"

Aljun'ra narrowed his eyes. He brought his hand down in a chopping motion, and three guards ran out the door.

Ryu managed to trip two of them neatly as they emerged. The third ran over the other two, oblivious to their grunts of pain, and made straight for Tabitha. He dove on top of her.

He probably thought it was a safe bet. Flexxent were large for aliens, and he was even larger than most Flexxent.

A moment later, however, his whole body shuddered and shot up in the air a foot or so before slamming down again heavily. It happened again. And again. Finally, he was hit so hard that he flipped over and landed heavily on his back.

Tabitha climbed to her feet and looked down at her shirt, where two holes marred the black cloth.

"This was one of my favorite shirts, jerkoff," she snarled. "You think it's *easy* to get new clothes out here?" With a sneer at the guards, she made her way into the lounge. "Let's find our guy."

Ryu followed with a soft sigh.

CHAPTER 5 TABITHA

"All right, everyone, listen up!" Tabitha came through the door with a swish of her coat and put her hands on her hips, scanning the room. "All...three of you. Where is everyone now?"

Benet Aljun'ra said nothing. He sat in the darkness and waited to see what this woman would say before he gave any more orders. His guards carried guns that were more than equal to the task of terminating this small human.

She was clearly wearing body armor, but that shouldn't matter. The rounds were armor-piercing.

When Benet gave an order to kill someone, they should have no chance of escape. The other three guards *should* have finished her off, but apparently, they'd gotten their asses handed to them outside.

To his annoyance, she looked up at him. She didn't seem thrown off by the darkness around his table.

"You run things around here?" Tabitha challenged him. "Or should I say, *were* you running things around here?"

"Kemosabe," Ryu muttered.

"He's a hack," Tabitha stated. She waved a hand at Benet in disgust. "Fancy suit, secluded table, sending guards out. We had a bunch of those in Buenos Aires. They aren't worth respecting."

Benet's lip curled. She was speaking Yollin—not the language of his people, but one he understood. She was clearly trying to provoke him.

"How may I help you?" He kept his voice pleasant.

There was no reason not to speak pleasantly, after all. As soon as he learned her purpose and any secrets he could about her armor and weapons, he would kill her. Meanwhile, he had a reputation to maintain as someone who *never* lost his temper.

"You can tell me where your guests went," Tabitha told him, annoyed. "I'm looking for Etoy Walce, and I *don't* suggest you stand between him and me."

"Mr. Walce is unknown to me. He was not on this evening's guest list."

Tabitha glared up into the darkness. She was willing to bet that this alien lied as often as he spoke. He'd probably figured out a way to lie without even saying anything.

"Listen up, chicken asswipe. I'm looking for this guy because he's been attacking supply ships for months and running off with things a lot of people, including some of his fellow Torcellans, require to do things like eat and build houses. If they've already got the goods, he kills them."

Benet sat back in his chair, bored.

"Okay, *don't* care," Tabitha snapped, annoyed. "You don't have to. You just have to tell me where he is. Or, should I say, you *want* to tell me where he is, because if you don't, life is about to get *very* unpleasant for you. I'm an Empress' Ranger, and I find those who knowingly shelter criminals to be just as culpable as—"

Benet gestured to one of the guards who had managed to stumble in from the street.

The guard may have just gotten the shit kicked out of him, but he knew better than to disobey an order from Benet. He shot Tabitha in the back at point-blank range, and she went skidding across the floor like a rag doll. The guard aimed again and shot Ryu as well.

"I had to shut the droning off," Benet explained from the darkness a moment after the tables stopped moving. "It was going on and on and on." He sighed. "I was getting bored."

Tabitha picked herself up off the floor and stared up into the darkness, her eyes flashing red. Her teeth began to lengthen.

"Then I'll make this a little less boring," she promised. She rounded on the guard. "I'm a Ranger. We try to arrest, but I think I'm good adding 'shoot me in the back' as a punishable-by-death offense."

———

Benet didn't wait to see how Tabitha planned to deliver on that threat. He was gone out a private door a moment later. It locked behind him with three deadbolts and two computerized locks with bioscanners and separate sixteen-digit codes. It opened into a reinforced tunnel that led to his private shuttle.

"That stuck-up sloth-brained monkey-tit twister!"

Tabitha yelled. "Ryu, after we clean up here, we're finding that ass!"

Ryu faced down a charging Flexxent and ducked, catching the alien at thigh level and flipping it over his head and onto the floor. He brought his foot up in a smooth arc and slammed it down on the alien's torso before kneeling to direct a punch at its face. "Yes, Kemosabe," he agreed calmly when he looked up.

"You're *definitely* Hirotoshi under there." Tabitha peered at him suspiciously. "I don't know how you pulled it off, but since when do *you* say, 'Yes, Kemosabe' in that stuffy tone?"

She took two steps and jumped at the guard who had shot her in the back. She kicked her leg out, and his head snapped back. He fell heavily to the ground, the gun falling from senseless fingers, and Tabitha stomped on his hand before looking back at Ryu.

"You and that needle-dicked suit up there would have a lot in common!"

Ryu's lips twitched as he tried not to let himself smile. Normally, he'd be throwing insults back, but now that he knew behaving like Hirotoshi annoyed her, he was going to keep doing it.

Her pain would be *priceless*.

One of the guards charged him with a yell, but he took the time to incline his head deeply to Tabitha.

"That's very hurtful, Kemosabe," he told her calmly. He ducked as the guards tripped over him, and sprawled on the floor. Ryu stood up, picked up one of the crystal tables, and slammed it down over the guard's body.

"I'm not sure…" She murmured.

Ryu did the same with another table just for good measure. "You can't be too careful, after all." The tables were so delicate, and the Flexxent were so very large.

Thankfully, after the second table, the guard didn't seem to be getting up.

Tabitha had hauled the guard who'd shot her into a big chair and was directing a series of punches at his face.

"Don't. Shoot. Me. In. The. Back!"

The chair collapsed and the guard went down with it, unconscious from the repeated hits. Tabitha picked up his gun and grimly shot him with it.

"Ugh. Jean has spoiled me for every other weapon."

"She would be most displeased to learn you even *used* anything else," Ryu said, drifting up behind her. He pretended not to notice the three remaining guards at the back of the room, who were preparing to charge. "Out of loyalty to you, Kemosabe, I will not tell her about this."

"Stop calling me that!"

"As you wish, Kemosabe!"

"Argh!" Tabitha waved her hands at him. "How are you doing this? How do you look like Ryu?"

"I *am* Ryu, Kemosabe." It was taking everything he had not to laugh. "Perhaps we should deal with the guards who are coming at us."

"Perhaps you should… I… You…" She glared at him. *"Pajero!"*

The two of them moved in unison, however, to head off the guards. Tabitha spun and brought her leg up, hitting one squarely in the middle of the chest. He wheezed and doubled over, fighting for breath. She grabbed him and used him to beat the second to the floor.

Ryu, meanwhile, dispatched the third with several precise strikes to Flexxent pressure points.

Sometimes reading Achronyx's full report was useful. "Should I mention knowing what they look like?" He shook his head. "Would instigate too much bitching."

"Let's finish this." Tabitha's eyes flashed as she strode toward the back room. "My favorite shirt is ruined, you're being a pretentious douche, and I got shot in the back! Etoy Walce, come out!" She ripped the door off its hinges and flung it into the room.

Several of the trapped guests screamed.

"Who is Etoy Walce?" one of them asked.

"A Torcellan who is not going to have any chance of—" Tabitha looked around. There were no other exits out of this room. "Is this everyone?"

"Why?" Ryu approached.

"Because there aren't any Torcellans here!"

Ranger Tabitha, I tried to inform you that you are in the wrong building. Etoy Walce was in the building next to this one.

"What do you mean, 'was?'"

He heard the gunfire and left.

Tabitha glared around the room. "Fine. We'll go find him, then!"

From behind them, someone cleared their throat. When Tabitha and Ryu turned, they saw a holo of Benet Aljun'ra, somehow looking both smug and annoyed.

"There is the small matter of damages," he asserted. "Before you leave, I will require a transfer of credits to cover the destruction of my property."

"The hell you will! Your guards shot me!"

"*After* you broke in." He gave a thin smile. "I assure you, you'll find that the law is quite clear on this point."

"*Ugh.* Achronyx, arrange it." Tabitha turned her nose up and swept for the door.

It's done, Achronyx reported as the doors swung open.

"Kemosabe." Ryu drifted up to her side unhurriedly as she marched down the street. "What's the lesson here?"

"Don't take Hirotoshi on missions. You distracted me and made me fall off the roof. I knew where I was when I was up there."

Ryu gave her a look.

"The lesson is to beat the shit out of the stuffed shirt, so he tells you the truth sooner."

"He *did* tell you the truth, Kemosabe. That's not the lesson."

"You aren't going to give up, are you? *Fine.* The lesson is to listen to your support team." She waved her hand disgustedly. "I get it."

They took a Pod up to the *Achronyx* in silence, Tabitha inspecting her shirt and making annoyed noises.

They had just stepped into the ship when Achronyx reported, "Ranger Tabitha, you have a call from Bethany Anne."

QBS Achronyx, Karkat spaceport

Tabitha arrived in her room to see Bethany Anne's call already onscreen. She sat on her throne, but her posture made it clear that this was an unofficial call.

Or *relatively* unofficial, at least.

"Glad I caught you," Bethany Anne began. "I only just

managed to get rid of the delegation from…whatsit. I don't remember. And there's another one coming in ten minutes."

"They're presenting a report on the Ixtali," John's voice said from off-screen.

"Hi, John," Tabitha called.

"Hi," he called back.

Bethany Anne got right to the point. "So, what's this transfer of credits into Karkat? You know," she added dryly, "the *exceedingly* large one."

"Oh, ah…" Tabitha managed a smile, but she was pretty sure it didn't look at all genuine. "Funny story—we went into this bar, right, looking for Walce, and this total asswipe told me he wasn't there and, well, to make a long story short, a lot of his bar got messed up and the law on their planet says that just because I broke in, I had to pay for everything. Even though he had people shoot me in the back!" she added indignantly.

Bethany Anne raised an eyebrow. "You broke in?"

"Well, they wouldn't let me in."

"Mmm. At least you got Walce."

"Oh." Tabitha cleared her throat. "About that. It turns out he wasn't there."

"This should be good," John remarked, his face now onscreen, leaning in from the right.

Tabitha glared at him. "How was I supposed to know?"

"You did mention that someone told you," Bethany Anne pointed out.

"You wouldn't have trusted a single word out of his mouth, either," Tabitha argued. "When I say 'total asswipe,' it is an insult to all asswipes. This guy was a whale douche of an asswipe."

Bethany Anne looked off into the distance for a moment, as if trying to make sense of what Tabitha had said, and she shook her head with a laugh.

"Tabitha, I sent you to get Walce, not support the rebuilding of their infrastructure—which we *will* do if we keep having to send payments that large."

"Right," Tabitha muttered.

"Just, you know, verify it next time. Have Achronyx look into it, maybe, so you don't have to believe the asswipe."

Tabitha cleared her throat again.

"What is it?" Bethany Anne sounded weary. "What did you do?"

Tabitha was many things, but she was not a coward. "Achronyx was trying to tell me he wasn't there."

Bethany Anne dropped her head into one hand. "Tabitha." It sounded like she was halfway between frustration and an attempt not to laugh.

"Okay, so Ryu—who might be Hirotoshi in disguise, actually—was talking about what it would look like if Barnabas cross-dressed and I fell off the roof, and then—"

Bethany Anne put up a hand. "*Tabitha!*"

Tabitha flushed. "Right. I'll be more careful."

"I don't object to your particular brand of havoc," Bethany Anne explained. "If I did, I wouldn't have made you a Ranger. However, next time try to make sure that if you mess up someone's bar, you don't have to pay them for it. And, you know, also try to get the person you're there for."

"Yeah." Tabitha nodded. "Sorry."

Bethany Anne grimaced. "I'm sorry too, but that's mostly because I have another meeting now. Go have fun for me. But…" She pointed at the screen.

"Not fun we have to pay thousands for. Yeah. I'll go get Walce."

QBS *Achronyx*, Meeting room

A half-hour later, at one of the docks outside Karkat, Tabitha sat in the *Achronyx's* main conference room, picking at her new shirt.

"It's just not as nice."

"It's the exact same shirt." Ryu sat down next to her. "You'd have to be insane to see any difference between them."

"It's a sentimental thing. I don't expect you to understand it." She replied. "This one is just okay. The *other* one was my favorite."

"So you *are* insane," Ryu muttered.

"Ha!"

"What?"

"I knew it! I knew the old Ryu was still in there! Insult my mom! Do it!"

Ryu stared at her. Finally, his lip twitched, and he started laughing.

"As much as I hate to interrupt," Achronyx said, "we do have Etoy Walce to find."

"Oh. Right." Tabitha lifted her eyes heavenward and took a deep, dramatic breath. "I suppose I should admit that I made some embarrassing mistakes at the lounge."

"You?" Ryu raised an eyebrow. "Embarrassed? Mistakes I'll admit, but *embarrassed*?"

"I am *trying* to work on my leadership skills, *Hirotoshi who looks like Ryu*, and it is important to admit things like this. As you encouraged me." She glared daggers at Ryu. "I should have listened to Achronyx when he tried to tell me that Walce was in the adjacent building. Had I done so, I would have apprehended him. And perhaps wouldn't have had to pay so many credits for property damage to that stuck-up prick."

Achronyx made a small whirring noise.

"Achronyx?"

"Since we are admitting our mistakes and embarrassment…"

"You want to rub it in, don't you? I'll have you know that my ego and pride are *almost* as large as my bodaciousness. I admitted to embarrassment, but I will not be admitting to anything more…" She paused a moment, "at least not yet."

"It wasn't your embarrassment to which I was referring, Ranger Tabitha." Achronyx made the sound again, as if one of his systems had hit a snag. "It happens that Etoy Walce was not the Torcellan who left the other bar during your altercation. He had checked out an hour before we arrived."

Tabitha frowned. "Wait, what?"

"I should have caught it," Achronyx admitted. "Had I done so, we would not be where we are now."

"Which is?"

"Trying to determine his present location. I should think that was obvious."

"I knew your politeness would only last so long," Tabitha muttered. She looked at Ryu. "And don't *you* have some things to apologize for?"

He stared at her for a moment, his eyes focused in concentration before he shook his head. "Not that I know of."

"Yes, you do." She jabbed a finger at him. "Achronyx and I admitted to our mistakes. You have to admit to yours."

"Agreed," Achronyx affirmed.

"But I made no mistakes that I am aware of," Ryu protested. "Of course, in Kemosabe's greater wisdom, she may know that I have—"

"*Stop being Hirotoshi! It's freaking the shit out of me!*"

Ryu leaned back. "I am sorry to have distressed you, Kemosabe."

"Dammit Ryu, you're insufferable! See, *that* was a mistake. You were behaving oddly during the mission."

"I was only trying to be polite," Ryu maintained innocently. "You often run such missions with Hirotoshi. Behaving as he does was, therefore, the best way *not* to distract you. And in any case, it is the best way to behave at all times."

She narrowed her eyes toward him.

"It is difficult to argue with him on that point," Achronyx allowed. "However, he did break multiple crystal tables."

"In service to Kemosabe, whose actions constituted implicit instructions to engage with the guards. It is my duty to make sure if someone attempts to attack her, they are incapacitated."

Tabitha stared at him. "Was that even English? You're talking like you're a thousand years old. Which I suppose you're close to."

Ryu smiled.

"I don't think we're going to get him on anything right now," Tabitha told Achronyx. "He has answers for everything. But he'll slip up sometime soon, I just know it. And we'll be ready, won't we?"

Yes, Ranger Tabitha, we will.

Ryu looked a bit unnerved. He was just opening his mouth when there was a ping on one of the systems and Achronyx announced, "It seems we have a new situation. There is a hit out on you, Ranger Tabitha, and it specifies this exact location."

"Who took it out?" Tabitha looked annoyed.

"That information is presently unavailable. The amount is fifteen thousand credits, sufficient to interest some of the more well-known assassins on Karkat."

"Fifteen *thousand*?"

"Yes, Ranger Tabitha."

"That's just insulting," Tabitha fumed. "Fifteen thousand. I've never been so humiliated in my life."

"Er…" Ryu cleared his throat. "Why, exactly?"

"It's tiny!" Tabitha glared. "They're trying to insult me."

"Having someone pay to have you killed is *insulting*?"

"They aren't paying to have me killed! That's not how much you'd pay to kill Ranger Two, it's how much you'd pay to kill…" Tabitha waved a hand in the air. "I don't know—your aunt if she didn't make your favorite birthday cake."

Ryu winced. "Well, that's just disturbing."

"Listen." Tabitha smacked the table angrily. "This guy has pissed me off. Achronyx, add to that news bulletin that the price has been raised to a hundred thousand."

Ryu's mouth hung open. "You cannot possibly be so egotistical that when someone takes a hit out on you, you get angry about the amount, and then you *add* to it to invite even more dangerous assassins to try to kill you!"

"Watch me!" Tabitha shot back. "Do you have any idea what kind of incompetent jackasses we'd get with fifteen thousand credits? Now we'll have some *real* challenges."

"I don't know if you're aware of this, but the conventional wisdom is that people trying to kill you is not ideal —especially when they're very, very good at it."

Tabitha crossed her arms and glared at him.

"It's not supposed to be a challenge to stay alive!" Ryu waved his hands. "Achronyx, back me up here."

"I am going to focus on getting us airborne." The EI replied. "I will leave you to explain these difficult-to-understand matters to Ranger Tabitha."

"Wait, what do you mean 'focus on getting us 'airborne'?" Tabitha frowned. "You do remember how to fly the ship, right?"

"Yes, but there appears to be some sort of liftoff restriction on the ship at present." A storm of beeping erupted from the monitors, and Achronyx sighed. "And now there are several inbound missiles."

"Let me talk to Flight Control!"

"I am connecting you, though, for the record, I am not sure how wise it is for you to talk to them. Perhaps Ryu should do so. Or me."

"Nuh-uh. Those missiles are coming for *me,* so *I* get to talk to flight control."

"They're coming for all of us," Ryu corrected.

"They're trying to kill *me.* You're just here." Tabitha sighed, annoyed, as the call connected. "Yes, hello. I'm trying to lift off at Dock 423, and there's a liftoff restriction on my ship."

"Yes, ma'am," a cultured voice replied. "It was placed there three minutes ago and will expire in approximately an hour."

"We need to go *now,*" Tabitha insisted.

"I'm sorry, ma'am, but you specifically requested that under no circumstances should we let your ship leave before an hour had elapsed."

"I didn't ask for that!"

"Our records indicate that you did."

"I didn't! It was not me!" Tabitha gripped the arms of the chair until they began to warp.

"Our records indicate—"

"I know what your records indicate, you inbred cretin! I am the captain of this ship, and I am telling you to let us lift off! There are four missiles inbound on our position."

"Ma'am, our records indicate—"

"Find me someone else!" Tabitha yelled at Achronyx.

At once, Ranger Tabitha. You will be connected in three... two...one—connected.

"Who is this?" Tabitha snapped.

"I beg your pardon?" a female voice responded.

"Then beg!"

"What?"

"Listen," Tabitha spat furiously, slamming her fist on

the table. "I am at Dock 423. Someone paid to put a lock on my ship and then sent four missiles at me. Flight Control is not letting me leave, which is a great plan if they were bribed but a less good plan when you consider that if those four missiles kill us, the explosion is probably going to take out all of your control buildings, too!"

"I see." The female voice sounded unconcerned. "I've lifted the restrictions on your ship. If you could make sure not to explode too close to the docks, it would be much appreciated."

Lifting off, Achronyx reported.

"I can't tell if I like her or hate her." Tabitha narrowed her eyes at the screen.

"I like her," Ryu offered. "Mostly because she got us out of here quickly."

"I would like to add," the female voice continued, "that I have given you return privileges to any of the city docks."

"See? She's nice." Ryu smiled at Tabitha. "Though I don't think we'll want to return."

"We'll just see about that. Achronyx, are you taking care of those missiles?"

In a moment. The ship shot directly up, and Achronyx spun them to face the four missiles that had altered their course as well and were climbing through the atmosphere. *Now that we're far enough from the docks, yes.*

A stream of pucks flew into the thinner air and made a beeline for the missiles. The four blew up one after another in an impressive set of double-explosions.

"Let's get somewhere else before we find out where Etoy Walce is," Ryu suggested. "And just think how much worse this would have been with a hundred thousand as the reward."

"Are you kidding? This was pathetic—and I am *not* going to be scared off. Achronyx, send that message raising the reward, and set us down outside Karkat."

Beside Tabitha, Ryu sighed.

Rebus Quadrant, Aboard the *Penitent Granddaughter*, Nickie's Quarters

Nickie.

She kept reading the words on her HUD, tuning out the interruption. If the interruption hadn't been inside her head, she might very well have plugged her ears and started humming.

Nickie!

Nickie jolted back to the present when the words on her HUD abruptly vanished, leaving her looking at the wall across from her bed. She blinked at it slowly for a moment before she realized that her communicator was beeping at her.

Based on Meredith's tone, it had probably been beeping for a little while. Nickie yanked it out of her pocket to answer it.

"Finally!" Grim exclaimed. "Look, you need to get over to the main hall. Sooner rather than later, preferably."

"What?" Even as she asked, she was already getting to

her feet. She grabbed her gun and her knife out of habit more than any belief that she would actually need either of them. "Why? What's going on?"

The door opened, and she jogged out of her quarters and through the corridors of the ship.

"Tensions are a little high, and everyone is sort of on edge. I don't think anyone really meant for it to get this far, and I'm pretty sure no one actually meant any harm—"

"Grim." Nickie cut him off before his nervous rambling could go on for any longer. "The short version," she demanded, nearing the airlock.

"Right." He cleared his throat sheepishly. "A fight broke out between a few of the colonists. Keen and I only have so many hands to break it up."

"Great." Nickie sighed, dragging her hand down her face. "I'll be right there." With that, she disconnected the call and broke into a jog.

Rebus Quadrant, Themis Colony

The weapons had been stacked and organized. The bots had been sent back to the ship. The injured had been tended to. The emotionally drained were asleep, slowly recuperating. The bodies of those they had all lost had been identified and moved so they could be given proper burials later. A few colonists had started cleaning up the blood coating so many of Tykis Outpost's walls, but only those who couldn't bring themselves to stop moving yet.

Everyone else had gathered in the main hall, where it seemed as if every distraction had already been used up.

Slowly, the adrenaline high that had carried them all out of the mines and kept them focused began to wane.

And as the energy drained, so too did any of the goodwill they had dredged up.

It was one of the maintenance workers, Tracy, who rounded on Keen, hands clenched at his sides as he shook with a mixture of exhaustion and outrage.

"So what do you have to say about all this?" Tracy demanded, closing the distance between him and Keen.

Keen heaved a slow, tired sigh. "What are you getting at?" He asked it so flatly that it didn't even sound like a question, and he didn't get up from his seat.

Tracy's hands clenched even harder, and he shook even more. "You're in charge of us. Under your watch, we were invaded, enslaved, and then invaded again before we even finished cleaning up after the first invasion. What are any of us supposed to think about that?"

"Hey, come on!" Melissa burst out, stomping forward to plant herself between Tracy and Keen. "How was he supposed to stop any of that? How was *anyone*?"

"Oh, I don't know. One woman managed to singlehandedly fight off two platoons of Skaines!" Tracy shouted back, throwing his hands up in exasperation.

A crowd was beginning to gather around them, murmuring amongst themselves as they tried to decide whether Tracy or Melissa was making more sense.

Melissa's mouth twisted to the side in irritation. "I'm pretty sure she's not a baseline human being," she pointed out sharply. "I mean, we all saw some of what she could do. Can you do any of that? Can *any* of us?"

Tracy scowled back, but he didn't have time to make a rebuttal before Jack chimed in. "Then maybe we shouldn't have come out to the ass-end of nowhere without any sort of defenses. None of us were trained for any of this."

"Oh, please." Harry scoffed, with a sharp bark of laughter. "What, should we have been sent with our own team of super-humans? Are you offering to pay for them out of your paycheck? Because you know damn well our company sure as shit ain't going to shell out for that sort of manpower."

"Then *he* should have fought for it!" Tracy barked, pointing one finger at Keen. "He should have fought for us!"

"You're being ridiculous, and you know it," Melissa snapped, folding her arms over her chest.

"Making even less sense than he usually does," Harry agreed dryly.

Grim inched his way over as they argued, coming to a halt beside Keen's chair. He fidgeted with his hands. "Should we...do something? Break them up or something like that?"

As if he had simply been waiting for that sort of cue, Tracy threw the first punch, his knuckles connecting with Harry's jaw with an audible impact. Harry stumbled back a few steps, one hand coming up to cup his jaw, before he charged forward a few steps to return the favor to Tracy, punching him square in the sternum.

Finally, Keen practically launched himself out of his chair, shouldering his way between the pair of them. He planted one hand on Tracy's chest and one hand on Harry's and pushed them away from each other, and then he refused to be budged from where he was.

If it hadn't been obvious enough that the cause of the

uproar was nerves and misplaced fear, it became painfully obvious then. Though Keen had been the initial target of the strife, even with him standing right in the middle of them, Tracy and Harry seemed more concerned with continuing to yell at each other. Though Melissa made a token attempt at getting Harry to calm down, it didn't take long before she and Jack were shouting just as loudly. Keen, in the middle of them, was left with little to do but keep them from ripping each other apart.

Grim pulled his communicator out and tried to connect a call. It felt like it rang for an eternity before Nickie answered and he filled her in on the situation.

It had seemed that everything was going so well until the shouting started. Clearly, the situation wasn't *good*, but it had appeared as though everyone had been more focused on trying to put everything back together. As he watched the mayhem unfold, he supposed it was only natural for tensions to run high.

He caught Melissa and Jack by their elbows when it looked like they were going to try to take their own shouting match even further. Even Keen was yelling by then, trying to get Tracy and Harry to screw their heads back on straight and act like rational human beings again. No one else needed to add more fuel to the fire.

"I would leave them to it," Grim cautioned, tugging Melissa and Jack away from the fracas. "No one needs either of you making the situation any worse."

Though Jack scowled at the perceived insult, Melissa simply shrugged as she silently conceded the point and took a few steps back. She couldn't go far, though. A rather impressive crowd had gathered around the arguing trio, making it impossible to get past without physically fighting through the wall of people.

Though only a few minutes had passed when the main doors opened and Nickie stormed in, Grim couldn't help but sigh in relief. Nickie breezed closer like a cloud passing over a field until she was elbowing her way into the middle of the crowd.

"That is enough!" she barked.

She slammed her way into the arguing knot shoulder-first, and Harry and Tracy both fell silent mid-shout as they stumbled away. Grim caught Keen as he backpedaled out of Nickie's path.

"I don't care who started it or why," Nickie growled. "I'm ending it. Whatever you're fighting about, it's not that important. It's definitely not important enough to start acting like the fucking Skaines, though I'm sure they would all be *thrilled* to see how you're behaving now."

The colonists seemed to wilt as one, growing quiet save for a few discontented murmurs. Still, Tracy gave one last valiant effort at making his point heard.

"But he—" Nickie leveled him with a glare that could have set a cruiser on fire. He closed his mouth so quickly he nearly bit the end of his tongue off.

"Bad things happen," she stated simply, though her tone brooked no argument. "This is not a just universe. You can do everything right and do your best at everything, and bad things *still* happen. It's no one's fault. No one caused it. It's just *life*."

Grim shuffled closer as he listened, glancing around at the colonists. None of them looked especially cheered by the dour speech, and even if it had stopped the argument, he wasn't sure if it was quite what any of them needed to hear just then.

But Nickie wasn't finished.

"Even if it was no one's fault—even if no one did anything wrong—that doesn't give you the right to be horrible to each other." She settled a meaningful look on Tracy and then on Harry. "Pinning it on a scapegoat won't make you feel any better. You don't get to be monsters because monsters found you. The only thing that's going to make you feel any better is proving that you're still better than those fuckers and that they haven't ruined the rest of your life. The only thing that's going to help is moving forward. You've all got legs. Use them."

She planted her hands on her hips and looked around. "Anyone else want to say anything?"

The crowd was conspicuously quiet after that. Nickie nodded once in satisfaction, and the crowd parted to let her walk away.

"Good. Now, at least some of you follow me so I can show you how those weapons work. They won't do much good if they just sit in storage."

Slowly, the others began to follow her as she walked away, like a chain of befuddled ducklings following the first adult duck they spotted.

Quite a speech.

Meredith sounded contemplative as she made the observation.

Yeah, well. It got them all to shut up.

Here I was hoping that you possibly believed that bit about it not being anyone's fault.

"This," Nickie began, holding a chrome spike with a red orb on top of it up like she was presenting it to royalty, "is a perimeter marker."

She slammed it toward the ground, sinking it into the dirt until the waist-height spike was only knee-high. "When it's active, the ball lights up. You line up a whole fuck-ton of them around whatever perimeter needs to be guarded."

She moved on, picking up a small turret. "This is, ah... perimeter permissions," she explained coyly, grinning when it at least got a few chuckles out of the group gathered around her. "If someone approaches the perimeter, the markers will catch them and alert the guard station, and whoever's on guard can tell the markers if they're welcome. If they are, they can pass through the perimeter just fine. If they *aren't* welcome, then the perimeter permissions," there she paused to waggle the turret in her hands, "will turn them into artisanal cheese."

She set the turret down and picked up a red orb about the size of a beach ball. "This is an atmospheric marker," she explained, holding it over her head. "You tell them how high to fly, and they monitor any ships that pass them and alert the guard station. If the ship has permission to be there or is otherwise benign, the guard does nothing and the ship lands safely. If the ship is hostile, the guard tells the markers, and the markers turn into bludgeons and crash into the invading ship as many times as it takes to wreck their shit."

She plonked it back down on the ground, planting one

foot on top of it to keep it from rolling away. It made a heavy, hollow *booooong* sound when she did. "These babies will follow the asswipe all the way down to the ground if they have to, and if that *still* doesn't dissuade them, they'll turn their attention to anything coming *off* the ship. You can even set them up to link up with the nearest perimeter markers if you really want to ruin someone's day."

She pulled her foot off the orb and stepped back, gesturing toward the various pieces to let the colonists investigate them. "They're all inactive and perfectly harmless right now unless you decide to hit each other over the head with them or some shit like that. Please don't."

You sound like you're having fun.

Little bit. It's nice to have a chance to distract everyone, at least.

So should I wait until later to give you the news?

Nickie meandered a few steps away from the colonists as Keen inspected the turret and Raynard tapped his knuckles on the atmospheric marker in academic curiosity.

What sort of news are we talking about?

I believe I've found a lead on the Skaines who made the retaliatory attack.

A clip from the colony's security footage of a Skaine cruiser landing appeared on her HUD. It was smaller than the previous two Skaine ships the colony had seen, but Nickie supposed if they had come with purely violent intent, it wouldn't take a lot of them of them to do a lot of damage.

The footage paused after only a few seconds and zoomed in on the name on the side of the ship.

"The *El'hana*," Nickie muttered under her breath, too

low for any of the colonists to hear her. Grim, though, was giving her a concerned look. Nickie flapped a hand at him and held a finger up a "one moment" gesture.

Think we could track it down?

Nickie folded her arms over her chest and began tapping her foot, antsy energy and the desire to get moving again already starting to flood her.

I believe so, yes.

That was all Nickie needed to know. She turned toward the colonists again, hands settling on her hips.

"All right!" she announced, louder than was strictly necessary to get everyone's attention. "Meredith will get with Raynard and make sure he has all the information he needs on how to set all these up and program them properly. This is where I leave you. I have a few chores to get out of the way."

Though the colonists seemed a bit leery about her leaving already, no one tried to stop her when she strode toward her ship with Grim loping after her.

Rebus Quadrant, Aboard the *Penitent Granddaughter*, Bridge

Nickie dropped into the command seat and propped her feet on Lucky's head. Grim stationed himself behind the first officer's console.

"Why the abrupt departure?" he asked, confusion evident in his tone. "Is there a problem?"

"Not necessarily a problem," Nickie replied. She glanced over her shoulder, spotting Durq lurking at his usual workstation. "You ever heard of the *El'hana*?"

Durq blinked at her dumbly for a moment before he finally replied. "Sort of? I-it was a while ago? All of my info would, uh, be, uh, out of date at best."

Nickie waved him off, unconcerned. "We'll check the job database, then. They're an active Skaine ship, which means they need to work, and that's the most convenient way for them to find work. Odds are we'll find them on there somewhere."

"I'll start looking," Meredith replied. The database

appeared at the edge of Nickie's vision, entries scrolling too fast for Nickie to register.

"What's the *El'hana*?" Grim asked, bemused. "Or is no one going to tell me what's going on here and why we're in such a hurry?" Already the ship was making the telltale growling noises that meant it was getting ready to take off. "And if anyone says 'it's a Skaine ship,' I will throw Brandy at you."

"It's the ship that invaded Themis after we left," Meredith answered.

Nickie scowled. "It's the ship piloted by the sons-abitches who killed eighty percent of the colonists," she added, vengefully. "And we're going to find those bastards and show them exactly what we think of what they've done." Her hands tightened into fists on her armrests.

"Oh," Grim replied faintly. "I see."

"Any objections?" she challenged.

"No, no," Grim mumbled in reply, staring down at the console in front of him. "I'm good."

The bridge was silent after that save for the sounds of the ship. It was a lot to think about, considering it was to be a revenge killing.

Meredith broke the silence. "The *El'hana* will be picking up a shipment of slaves in three days. I suspect they will need to lie low beforehand, both to restock and to prevent anyone from catching on to what they're doing." The database on Nickie's HUD scrolled rapidly to the proper entry. "Of the handful of viable locations for them to stop before they begin their job, I suspect that Vanquisher Space Station is the most likely."

"What makes Vanquisher so special?" Nickie asked even

as she confirmed the coordinates to begin heading in its direction.

"It's near the colony their job is on, and it has considerably more amenities than Ravager or Shelloc Station," Meredith replied. "It will allow them to refuel and restock while also allowing them to remain anonymous in comfort."

Nickie nodded absentmindedly in agreement. "Vanquisher it is, then," she mused. "We can kick their asses for what they did on Themis and what they're trying to do now. It'll be a two-for-one deal."

Grim drummed his fingers on his console. "We're sure these are the Skaines who attacked the colony?"

"Positive," Meredith assured him.

"It sounds like something the captain would do," Durq added, although it sounded like he was mumbling it to himself.

"That's settled, then," Nickie decided, nodding once as if to close out the argument. She stretched her arms over her head and arched her back away from the seat before slumping back into it, her arms landing on the armrests once again.

Grim watched her quietly for a few minutes. At first, it seemed as if she were focusing on the main viewing screen with almost single-minded intensity, until it became apparent that her thoughts were a thousand miles away.

Slowly, he moseyed over to the command chair, stopping beside it.

"Credit for your thoughts?" he asked. Nickie jerked in surprise as she snapped back to the present. She looked up at him sharply, and Grim had to pull his mandibles tight to his mouth to keep from laughing at her reaction.

She swatted at him half-heartedly with the back of one hand. "Asshole."

Grim was beginning to think she was simply going to keep her thoughts to herself when Nickie suddenly glanced around and motioned for him to come closer. He leaned down to hear her when she started to speak.

Nickie's voice was low so Durq wouldn't hear her from across the bridge. "We need to get rid of the Skaines. Just… all of them. They need to be done. Gone. Over with. Every last fucking one of them. None of them can be expected to be civilized at this point."

She was calm as she said it, as if she had simply come to an ordinary, everyday conclusion. "These ones are just going to be first."

Grim shifted uncomfortably. "What about the ones who were selling weapons to the Leath?" he asked slowly. "I mean, you did promise Molly you would handle them."

Nickie waved it off, unconcerned. "They fall into the category of 'all the Skaines,'" she pointed out, sounding a bit too reasonable for the decision she was making. "We can get to them later. Molly and I aren't exactly old and decrepit. I'll have plenty of time to keep my promise to her."

Grim nodded slowly in agreement. "All right," he replied after a moment. "If you're really set on doing that, I'm not deluded enough to think I can change your mind."

Nickie grinned up at him. "I always knew you were clever."

On any ordinary day, the bar would have been pretty quiet. It wasn't the fanciest bar on the station, but it wasn't the plainest, either. As a result, it tended to attract a very in-the-middle sort of crowd.

On most days.

Today it was full of Skaines who were all high from a job well done and eager to tell everyone about it, regardless of the fact that no one else in the bar wanted to listen to them.

"And so I says to the guy... Do you know what I said to him?" Belk rumbled out an unsteady laugh, and his whiskey slopped over the side of his glass. If nothing else, at least the loudest of them were too drunk to realize that no one was paying attention to them.

"We all know wha—" Gern broke off to hiccup, then threw back the last of his drink. "What you said," he finished, slamming his empty glass onto the bar top. "We've heard this story, like...four trillion times."

Belk butted his head against Gern's, sending him pitching sideways off his stool. "I barely had time to-to tell it *twice*," Belk insisted before he finished his whiskey. He emphasized his words by picking up his glass and giving it another purposeful thump. "Hey. Heyyyyyy," he repeated louder, waving his empty glass over his head like a banner. To say he was slurring didn't do his tone justice.

By the time one of the bartenders made her way over, she had long since given up on even pretending to be pleasant, instead eying the puddles the pair of them had slopped on the bar. And that wasn't even getting into the rest of the Skaines who had taken over half the bar. She was pretty sure they had broken at least three of the chairs since their arrival.

"More of the same?" she asked flatly. From the corner of her eye, she could see her coworker fetching a mop from the closet.

"Make mine a double this time," Gern interrupted, scrambling awkwardly back onto his stool. It had been designed for someone several inches taller than him, but he seemed unperturbed.

"Yeah, yeah, that sounds good," Belk agreed eagerly, waggling his empty glass in the bartender's face.

With heroic willpower, she refrained from rolling her eyes at them before she took their empty glasses away and brought them their refills.

Belk downed a quarter of his refill in a couple of gulps, liquor slopping down the corners of his mouth. "Hey, d-do *you* want to know what I said to the guy?" he asked, leaning as far over as he could to talk to the woman at the other end of the bar.

She looked like she would rather be anywhere else in the world, and she stared down intently at her beer and her wrist holo. She asked, "What'd you say?" only because it seemed like a faster way to get him to leave her alone than ignoring him or telling him to get lost.

Belk wobbled on his stool and grabbed the edge of the bar to keep himself from toppling to the floor. "I-I said 'this is what happens when slaves don't know their goddamn place,' and then I ripped his throat out and left him on the floor."

The woman flinched and hunched over her wrist holo

as if Belk would simply disappear if she pretended he wasn't there hard enough. Both bartenders went still and shared an uneasy look, but they both already knew that station security didn't have much of a say in what the Skaines did if they didn't actually do it on the station.

Belk eyed the woman until it was incredibly obvious that she wasn't going to say anything. He scoffed and leaned away, grumbling to himself before he took another gulp from his glass.

Gern elbowed Belk sharply, and his voice was too loud when he said, "Aw, come on, that's nothing."

"If you got something better, then share it," Belk challenged, glowering at him petulantly.

"I found one of those, uh…those spike things they use for…some shit in the mines, I don't know. I don't do peasant work." He waved it off, unconcerned, before he held his hands up a good foot apart. "That big. Kinda rusty. Still pretty sharp. And I-I cornered a guy in a storage room, and he was blubbering like a little bitch, all snotty and loud, and I ripped his throat with the spike. A-and then, before he'd died, I nailed him to the wall with the spike-whatever-it-was. Modern art, if you ask me." He lifted his drink and downed it in one go before slamming his glass back down and belching. He laughed belatedly, evidently oblivious to the fact that half of the bar's occupants were trying very hard to pretend that he wasn't speaking.

He leaned over and elbowed Belk again. "See? Bet you can't top that."

"Don't touch me," Belk groused, swatting Gern's arm away and emptying his glass again. Before he could demand another refill he wobbled, and with a startled shout, he tipped over backward and tumbled off the stool to land in a heap on the floor. With a groan, he lifted an arm to paw at the stool before deciding that getting back up was just too much work.

A moment later there was a snore, loud, soggy, and not entirely unlike a fog horn. Gern squinted down at him and jiggled his stool side-to-side for a few seconds, purposely bonking Belk in the side of the head with one of the stool's legs. Belk didn't stir and kept on snoring.

With a shrug, Gern picked up Belk's mostly empty glass and drained the dregs of it before slamming it back down to the bar top again.

With his company suddenly considerably worse at carrying on a conversation, Gern hopped down from the stool and wobbled toward the door. He got halfway there before he remembered that he should probably pay.

"My tab's on him," he decided, flapping a hand in Belk's direction before he went out the door. He nearly walked into a support beam five feet away from the bar.

Rebus Quadrant, Vanquisher Space Station

We have permission to dock. I assume you are ready to disembark.

I've been ready since we set the coordinates.

Meredith made no response to that, so Nickie simply checked her weapons one last time and headed for the airlock. She met Grim halfway there, and he trotted after her for a few steps before catching up and slowing to a walk.

He followed her in silence as they made their way off of

the ship, out of the docking bay, and farther into the station. It wasn't like Minerva Outpost, which had been designed to make people want to shop and spend money. Instead, Vanquisher was comparatively utilitarian. While individual locations were as dolled up as could be, the station itself looked almost industrial, with beams, supports, and struts bared. The flooring was simply metal tiles, and all that had been covered were the aspects that had to be hidden for safety. There weren't even any windows except in specific businesses.

It wasn't the most cheerful place to stay, but it did its job well enough, and the fact that it wasn't particularly pretty didn't seem to have kept anyone away from it.

It wasn't long before Nickie and Grim came upon a bar, only just far enough from the docking bay that it couldn't be accused of encouraging irresponsible behavior. Small and reasonably unadorned, it didn't stand out particularly from any other bar, despite its decidedly grandiose name.

They came to a halt a few meters from the bar, and a cursory glance made it clear that there weren't many Skaines inside at that point. There were a few, but the majority of the patrons were Yollin and Zhyn, with a smattering of humans.

Most notably, though, there were two rather inebriated Skaines right outside the bar, slumped in front of a support beam. They were grumbling at each other and pushing each other halfheartedly. They were barely even conscious.

Nickie gave them a brief once-over before deciding that they would do, and she took off at a jog toward them, forcing Grim to keep up.

She dropped to a crouch in front of the two Skaines

and grabbed one by the front of his shirt. She hauled him close and gave him a shake, and when that didn't get enough of a reaction, she slapped him across the face.

"Go awaaaay." He groaned, flailing a hand at her without much luck. "Sleepiiiiiing."

Nickie punched him, which seemed to wake him up. He blinked several times and scowled at her as he slurred, "What d'ya want? We didn't do nothing."

"I'm looking for the crew of the *El'hana*," Nickie replied, and she gave him another harsh shake when it looked like he was contemplating drifting off again.

His companion replied, grumbling almost inaudibly, "Ship left. Not here anymore." He flapped a hand at Nickie and rolled over as if the support beam he was leaning against was as comfortable as a pillow.

Granted, given what Nickie knew of Skaine home decorating, maybe it was.

"Fuck off," the Skaine still dangling from Nickie's hold contributed intelligently. "We didn't do shit." He squiggled in a manner that was maybe supposed to be intimidating, but given his lack of coordination, it came across more like a cat trying to get out of a sweater.

For a long moment, Nickie stared at them both. Maybe they weren't part of the *El'hana*'s crew, but they were still Skaines. It seemed like a sure bet that they had done *something* to get them into trouble at some point or another. It was what the Skaines did, after all.

She let go of the front of the Skaine's shirt, and her fingers curled into a fist, tight and bloodless. They were both so drunk they would hardly be able to do anything, and she doubted they would even remember her face by the time they sobered up. It wouldn't be a big deal.

Grim grabbed her shoulder and she jolted in surprise, dropping the Skaine back to the floor as she did. She stared up at Grim blankly, as if she had completely forgotten he was there.

Slowly, as if he were trying to negotiate with a mountain lion, Grim asked, "Since we aren't going to find what we're looking for here, how about we get a drink?" He motioned to the bar behind them with one hand.

With stiff, mechanical movements, Nickie looked at the bar and slowly straightened back up to her full height. "Right. A drink," she agreed belatedly, before she pivoted on her heel and walked into the bar. Grim glanced back at the Skaines as he followed her, but they were both already drifting off again, still grumbling. As he watched, a Yollin stepped over them while hurrying on her way.

As they stepped into the bar, Grim could just barely hear one of the Skaines mumble, "I think we almost got mugged by a bounty hunter." Grim shook his head and shoved the pair of them out of his mind for the time being.

Nickie snagged a stool at one end of the bar, and Grim stood and folded his arms on the top. One of the bartenders stopped in front of them with a cordial, "What'll it be?"

"Whiskey," Grim replied. "Yollin, if you have it. No ice, and don't be stingy."

"I've had a really bad day," Nickie added. "Surprise me."

The bartender's eyebrows rose, but he didn't comment as he walked away. Evidently, it wasn't the first time such a request had been made, since as he returned just a few moments later with a pair of glasses. Grim's drink was the familiar amber of whiskey, but Nickie's was possibly the most violent shade of green either of them had ever had seen.

"Bottoms up," the bartender offered as he set their drinks down, before moving down to the other end of the bar to tend to the Zhyn who was trying to flag him down.

Nickie gave her drink a slightly dubious sniff, but it was the only sign she offered that she wasn't quite sure what it was. If she cared, she offered no indication of it. In fact, she offered no real indication of anything that was on her mind just then.

Grim could hazard a guess. Between her taking off into the mines, the speech she had delivered to the colonists, and the close call she'd had with the drunken Skaines, he was pretty sure it was the least in control of her emotions she had been in quite some time.

He offered no comments on the matter, though. Instead, when she finally picked up the shot glass to cautiously sip it, Grim held his glass out expectantly. Nickie eyed his glass for a second before rolling one shoulder in a lazy shrug and tapping the rim of her glass against his. It made a quiet ringing sound, and she pulled her glass close again.

After one last wary sniff, she took the smallest possible sip from her drink and recoiled slightly as soon as it touched her tongue. Grim masked his laughter behind the rim of his glass. Not fooled for an instant, Nickie scowled at him, but it was halfhearted at best.

She didn't *dislike* the drink, though, even if the strength of it was enough to sweep her legs out from under her. As if to prove that it couldn't best her, she threw her head back and downed it in one quick gulp.

It burned all the way down, but it was a pleasant, familiar sort of burn. It left her feeling like she was buzzing after just one shot of it. Knowing it was probably a bad idea, she couldn't help but contemplate asking for another.

Grim sipped his drink at a more sedate pace. As if he could read her thoughts, he cleared his throat. "Please don't make it so I'll have to carry you back to the ship," he requested dryly. "It will be embarrassing for both of us."

With a snort, Nickie punched his shoulder with her free hand. Still, she had to admit that it *was* probably a bad idea to go for seconds. There was relaxing, and then there was being a sloppy drunk. The latter didn't sound appealing.

He didn't seem inclined to talk after that, and she didn't feel much of a need to break the silence as he finished his drink. She felt calmer by then, or less ready to let her fists fly, at any rate. There was a time and a place for giving Skaines what for, after all. Nothing good would come of it if she decided to throw down with every incidental Skaine she saw.

Vigilantes were supposed to fight for Justice, after all. They weren't supposed to fight just because it felt good to fight.

CHAPTER 8 NICKIE

Rebus Quadrant, Aboard the *Penitent Granddaughter*, Bridge

As the ship undocked and prepared to leave the space station, Nickie stared at the quadrant map that had taken over most of the main viewing screen. Her elbows were on her knees, and her fingers were steepled in front of her chin. Grim was in the kitchen, and Durq was probably helping him. Nickie was alone with her thoughts.

"So if they aren't *here,*" she groused, scowling at the map, "then where the fuck are they?" The map offered her no answers or explanations.

Meredith's reply was matter-of-fact. *The Skaines you questioned said they had left, so clearly they* were *there.*

Which means they'd already restocked and were headed elsewhere to lay low. There are a few likely options in the general area. Which one seems the most likely?

Nickie asked the question without taking her attention from the map, her patience already beginning fray at the edges. Meredith wasted no time.

The map shifted, highlighting and then zooming in on a specific system and then one planet in particular.

This is Swapayama. Technically speaking it is a human colony, but it's very sparsely populated and has only a few villages.

Atmospheric readouts and population density reports appeared at the edge of the map.

The atmosphere is habitable for the Skaines, and the colony is not advanced enough to notice if they have company, as long as the Skaines do not announce their presence. They can remain undetected until it is time for them to complete their job.

Nickie slumped down in her seat and scuffed one boot against the floor.

Great. Just what we need. A shipful of hostile Skaines hiding on another human colony. Because that definitely didn't fuck everyone over the last few times it happened. Skaines and humans go together like oil and water.

We'll be there shortly. There's no sense in getting worked up about it already.

Well, plot a course, then. I want to be there, like...yesterday.

I'm afraid time travel is a bit outside this ship's capabilities, but I will come as close as I can.

Nickie grumbled, less actual words and more just indistinct nonsense syllables to make her displeasure with the entire situation known. Her displeasure was not subtle. Everyone was aware of it.

She levered herself reluctantly upright in the command chair before getting to her feet. She stretched, reaching over her head and arching backward until her spine popped, then headed toward the door.

I'll be busy once we make it to Swapayama. I'm going to go shovel down some food and get ready. Last thing we need is to be caught with our pants down and our asses hanging out on some backwater little spit of a colony.

With that decision made, she left the bridge. Meredith would let her know once they were close enough to start worrying. In the meantime, she had other things to think about, and someone had to let Grim know what was going on.

Rebus Quadrant, Regleon System, Planet Swapayama

The community center had been the heart of the village for years. Building it had been a community event, not unlike a barn raising, and nearly everyone attended parties and celebrations in it at least a few times a month. It was a simple building, but well-loved all the same.

A Molotov cocktail arced through the air toward it, hitting the roof of it and erupting into flames. Three more followed, one of them landing in the doorway and blowing the main door off of its hinges.

Finally, a grenade smashed through one of the windows, and when it exploded, it took out an entire corner of the building.

It was just a bit of light entertainment as far as the Skaines were concerned. Most of the villagers had fled into the underground shelter as soon as they saw the *El'hana* landing outside the village. They were just flushing out the last few who hadn't managed to make it into the shelter.

If nothing else, it was a good excuse to let off a bit of steam before they had to buckle down to work, and they had managed to find some unexpected goodies as they made their way through the largely empty village.

A good evening, all things considered. A good way to get ready for the next job.

With a roar of laughter, seven Skaines slammed their weight against a shed until the thing gave up on staying upright. With a groan and a series of cracking sounds, the wood conceded. One wall cracked and fell forward, and the rest of the shed tipped to the side in one piece before breaking apart.

There were two girls huddled together in the space where the shed had been. The older of the two was only in her early twenties. The younger one couldn't have been older than sixteen. They clung to each other as they waited for the Skaines to kill them. They probably would have preferred for that to happen.

Instead, Gern laughed and grabbed the older one by the hair. She shrieked and stumbled after him on all fours as he started pulling her away, until she managed to trip her way to her feet. With her head cocked at an odd angle to try to minimize how hard he was pulling, she followed behind him.

"Trina!" the younger one shrieked even as she scrambled up to her feet and got ready to run. She only made it a few steps before Belk tackled her into the dirt, his arms around her middle. She screamed and flailed, thrashing like a fish on a line, but it didn't do any good. His grip was too strong, and it seemed like it took zero effort for him to get back to his feet and sling her over his shoulder like a sack of flour.

As he carried her away, she could see the hatch that led into the community shelter. Even from a distance, she could tell it was locked. There was no way to open it from the outside. Even if she had managed to make it over there, there was no way anyone below would hear her shouting. Even if they did, they wouldn't get it open before the Skaines scooped her up again.

She tried to be grateful that her friends and family were safe, or at least most of them were. She could see a few bodies on the ground near where the community center was burning. She tried not to be jealous or resentful of the fact that she had been locked out and abandoned. If she was going to die in the next few hours, she didn't want to die angry.

Belk adjusted the way he was carrying her, shifting her weight and jolting her back to the present, even if that was the last place she wanted to be.

She kicked and flailed and thrashed the entire way back to the ship, her fists hammering ineffectually against Belk's back. He didn't even seem to notice, and he didn't let her go until he dumped her on the ground beside the ship on the far side of the Skaine encampment.

She landed in a heap and immediately tried crawling toward the woods. She could lose them in the trees and make a mad dash for the next village over.

She only made it a couple of feet before Belk planted a foot against her shoulder and kicked her back. She landed on her backside beside the other girls, and a moment later all six of them were chained together by their wrists. He sank one end of the chain into the ground like he was tethering a dog, and with a harsh laugh that sounded more like a growl, he patted her on the head and made his way back to the festivities.

She looked around quickly to see if there was something

—anything—she could use to break the chain, but there was nothing there. She didn't even have enough space to get her hands free by breaking her thumbs. As drastic as that sounded, it was a sacrifice she was willing to make just then.

"Kelly, there's no use," one of the others told her, but she shook her head quickly. There had to be *something* she could do.

She threw her weight forward to try to rip the chain free of the dirt. All she managed to do was fall over sideways onto the ground, her arms at an awkward angle. She squirmed and yanked on the chain for a few more minutes until she exhausted all of her energy and went limp in the grass. She stayed there, chest heaving as she tried to catch her breath, but she couldn't quite manage to do it.

It felt like she couldn't get enough air into her lungs. One of the others was petting her hair, but it sort of felt like it was happening to someone else. Her chest felt too tight, her head hurt, and each breath felt like she was trying to draw it past a stone in her throat.

She curled into a ball as much as she could just then, pulling her arms up to hide her face as she sobbed. She didn't know what was going to happen to her or to Trina or the others, but she had a feeling she wasn't going to see her friends or her family again after that night. She wasn't even sure if she would still be alive by morning, and if she were, she wasn't sure she would want to be.

She tried to stop thinking about it, tried to get her thoughts to go blank. But her mind kept churning, toiling over every horrible thing that could happen. She wanted to go home.

She was still curled on the ground when Gern and Belk returned, just to make sure that none of them had found a way to escape. Belk gave the chain one more tug before letting it go, satisfied that it would hold for as long as they needed it to.

"So, which one's your favorite?" he asked dryly, looking over his shoulder at Gern.

"Are we calling dibs on them now?" Gern asked in return, brows rising. "Captain's probably not going to like that."

"It's an academic question," Belk returned. "The captain doesn't need to know. And the captain doesn't need six of them, anyway."

"The small one, I guess," Gern replied, shrugging one shoulder. "The others are too tall. It's rude."

"I'm taller than most of them," Belk pointed out with a grin.

"Rude," Gern insisted before he kicked a clump of dirt at him. "Not sure I actually like any of them, though," he added. "Are humans always this noisy?"

All six of them were crying by then, watching him and Belk like they were waiting for their throats to be torn out. They were making that idea more appealing with each passing second. Really, all that sniffling just seemed unnecessary. It was *rude*.

"Pretty sure it's just a human thing," Belk replied, unconcerned. "We can gag them or something later on. I wouldn't worry about it."

Gern gave one of them a poke with his boot, but that only made it worse. She squealed for a second and tried to skitter away from him, and it sounded like she was hyper-ventilating. It was all enough to make his head ring.

"Uugh." Gern groaned in exasperation, and he clapped a hand over the nearest girl's mouth. "Enough with that gods-awful noise," he snapped. Despite that, she kept sniffling and whimpering, and the rest of the girls were crying now. One of them started sobbing behind her hands.

Gern's free hand closed into a fist, but before he could get any more annoyed, Belk grabbed his shoulder. "Come on, we're going to miss dinner," Belk whined, practically dragging Gern away from the girls. "We found all kinds of good shit in a few of the basements. And you wouldn't believe what sort of moonshine these hicks have been brewing, and I'm punting you off a cliff if I miss it. We haven't had a good meal since our cook got eaten by a carnotaur."

Gern reluctantly let himself be dragged away, though he could still hear the girls whining like spoiled mutts behind him. The idea of gagging them was tempting. Or maybe just stapling their mouths shut. It wasn't like they were going to need them, after all.

They were going to be there for a little while, though. Long enough to come up with some fun ideas, at any rate. He could find a way to get the lot of them to shut the hell up later. He could probably even make it fun. Maybe Belk would help him.

Belk gave his arm another impatient tug, and Gern put the girls out of his thought for the time being. He gave the back of Belk's head a slap and declared, "Last one there gets the gristle." He broke into a sprint with Belk shouting at him from right on his heels.

Gern had a feeling it was going to be a pretty good night.

Rebus Quadrant, Aboard the *Penitent Granddaughter*, Bridge

For the most part, space always looked quiet and gentle. Even when things collided, it always looked as if it were happening in slow motion. When bad things happened on the ground, they were invisible from space. Like with an ant farm, most things were invisible until someone actively chose to look, and that didn't happen too often.

Nickie watched Swapayama get closer on the main viewing screen. Swapayama looked quiet just then. It looked gentle, with its three moons orbiting it in silence, the tides in its oceans churning, and the clouds swirling through the atmosphere like they were doing their own ballet.

Did the Skaines' homeworld look gentle from the vantage point of space? It probably did. Regardless of who the Skaines chose to be, a planet was just a planet, and it probably looked just as quiet as Swapayama or Themis.

Nickie couldn't really imagine that. In her mind's eye, it was always on fire, with the Skaines too busy fighting everything and anything to put the fires out. She knew she could just look up a picture or a video of it, but she didn't really want that mental image to be corrected just then.

Swapayama looked like any other colony from so far away, but based on the reports Meredith was giving her, Nickie knew that looks could be deceiving.

There is a distress signal coming from one of the outer villages. So far the trouble seems to be localized to that area, and it would seem that most of the village is sequestered in a bunker. However, there have been casualties and considerable structural damage.

What are the odds of the trouble spreading to the other villages?

The Skaines seem disinclined to head elsewhere at the present moment, but the closest villages have gone underground preemptively. These people are not combatants, and they are all aware of that.

How primitive are these bunkers, anyway? How much abuse can they take?

It is possible that the Skaines could break through if they put in enough effort, but that doesn't seem particularly likely at this time. If they are just here to blow off steam before moving on to their next job, I would not put money on them expending more effort than they absolutely have to.

Nickie wasn't particularly comforted by that assurance. Being told "oh, they could cause as much damage as they want to, they're just too lazy right now" wasn't exactly what she would call good news.

We'll be landing soon?

Correct.

Nickie nodded, arms folded over her chest as she drummed her fingers on her elbows. She had made most of her preparations already, and Grim and Durq were staying behind on the ship, so they didn't need to get ready. Durq was lurking at the communications terminal in the unlikely event that they needed to call for help. Nickie wasn't sure where Grim was.

As if on cue the door slid open, and Nickie peered over her shoulder as Grim stepped onto the bridge.

"Ready for all of this?" he asked mildly, coming to a halt beside her. He watched the main viewing screen for a moment.

"As ready as I can be," Nickie confirmed, shrugging loosely. "Have fun holding down the fort while I'm out there."

He snorted out a quiet laugh. "Right." His tone sobered after that, though, as he wondered, "Are you sure you want to do this?"

Nickie slid him a narrow sidelong glance. "What are you getting at, Grim?"

"Are you sure you want to go storming out there while you're still pissed off at the universe?" he asked, folding his arms and turning to face her fully. "Just—" He sighed and shook his head. "I don't want anything bad to happen, is all. A lot could go wrong here."

Nickie glowered up at him. "Relax," she snapped, planting her hands on her hips. "I know exactly what I'm doing, and I don't need anyone lecturing me on how to do it. Especially not you. So lay off."

Grim didn't rise to the bait. He was already tired from the direction the conversation had turned.

"Will you at least promise me that you won't do anything drastic?" He sighed, rubbing the back of his head with one hand. "These colonists need help, but nothing good will happen if you start doing things you'll regret later." He put a bit more feeling into his voice as he reminded her, "You weren't the one who landed the El'hana on Themis, and going crazy here won't undo what happened."

Nickie's eyes narrowed sharply for a few seconds

before she let her expression ease back to chilly neutrality. "Considering I doubt you'll be giving me much help while we're here, I don't really think any of what you have to say matters that much." Her eyebrows rose expectantly. "Or am I wildly off-base here?"

Before he could help it, Grim let out an incredulous laugh. It wasn't a particularly pleasant sound. "Yeah, that's kind of what I was talking about," he mused dryly. "But if that's how you want to play it, far be it from me to argue. Just try to remember that no one on this ship is your enemy or you won't have anyone left to clean it up when you finish turning yourself into a bottle rocket."

He didn't wait for her to say anything else, just left. Durq followed him for a few paces, then paused. Maybe he wanted to say something, but he thought better of it when Nickie punched the back of the command chair with enough force to dent it. Durq scuttled away before she could turn her ire on him, disappearing underneath his usual console.

Nickie growled and threw her hands into the air, then turned back to the main viewing screen.

Fuck both of them. What did they even know? They weren't the ones throwing themselves into the fight all the time.

Rebus Quadrant, Regleon System, Swapayama, Aboard the *Penitent Granddaughter*, Bridge

Entering the planet's atmosphere was about as uneventful as it could be. There were no messages or demands to know who they were or anything like that. If the Skaines weren't expecting anyone to show up and the colony wasn't advanced enough to have perimeter sensors, it was no surprise that no one noticed them arriving.

The main viewing screen changed to a mishmash of reds and oranges and yellows surrounded by the darker, cooler blues of trees and bushes. The nearest village was easily visible, and farther away the Skaines were gathered around the cool blue of their ship. There was a small cluster amongst the Skaines, just a shade paler. Humans, but only a few.

Based on the difference in temperature, I believe the Skaines have taken six of the colonists of the nearest village hostage. There will be extensive damage to the village as well, but I would recommend prioritizing those six.

It wasn't even remotely surprising, but Nickie could feel a surge of exasperation welling up in her chest all the same. She groaned and dragged one hand down her face. She let her head thump back against her seat, only to sit back up with a jerk when she hit her head on the newly-acquired dent.

I knew this was going to happen. They're halfling-sized. How do they always manage to take so many hostages?

They are adept at attacking colonies that have limited defenses. You already know that. It's not the colonists' fault for getting captured.

Nickie didn't reply at first, scowling down at the floor between her boots. Finally, she got to her feet and changed the topic entirely.

When we land, I want to be far enough away that they won't see us immediately, but not so far that it will take me too long to get there.

I will land the ship on the far side of the grove. If there are any preparations you still need to make, now is a good time to do so. I will begin landing procedures shortly.

Nickie hummed absently in agreement and turned toward the door. She had her drones in her belt pouch already, and she could check that her gun was in working order on her way to the airlock.

By the time the ship landed on the far side of the trees, Nickie was already standing at the airlock. Grim didn't put in an appearance to wish her luck, and Nickie scowled down the corridor as if he would see the look on her face. With a wordless groan of irritation, she turned toward the airlock and made her way off the ship.

The light was dim once she was standing at the edge of the grove. She could make out the hazy glow of the Skaine encampment if she looked through the trees at the right angle, but it wasn't enough to see by—not that she really needed the light. A grid laid itself over her vision, outlining every tree, rock, and root.

Nickie took a step into the woods, then broke into a sprint, weaving through trees. It was as simple as walking down a sidewalk at midday, and she put on an extra burst of speed after a few yards.

There was probably a kilometer of forest between the *Penitent Granddaughter* and the *El'hana*. For anyone else, through the dark and the trees and on unfamiliar terrain, it would be at least a twenty-minute trip. Longer, probably.

Nickie's long strides ate up the ground like they were hungry for it, legs pounding like pistons. Within six minutes she was nearly through the trees, and she wasn't even winded. As far as she was concerned, it might as well have been a leisurely evening jog.

She scaled a tree while she was still hidden enough to do so, and as she got higher off the ground, the grid over her vision stretched out farther and farther. She crept to the end of the branch, balanced on her toes. But as far as she could see, nothing and no one was coming toward the woods. No one had noticed her or heard anything.

Granted, she could hear the ruckus the Skaines were making, and she could smell their bonfires and their booze from her position. She was pretty sure she could have danced naked backed by a full brass band, and they still wouldn't have noticed her.

She wasn't going to complain.

She hopped down from the branch, landing in a crouch in the grass before straightening to her full height. She kept moving forward, and when she was close enough for the light of the Skaine encampment to give her good visuals, the grid over her vision vanished. She could hear them laughing and shouting and telling stories, and she wanted to beat all their faces. Then none of them could tell stories like nothing was wrong while they had hostages tied up on the other side of their ship.

But that was what she was there for. Maybe she wouldn't beat their faces in, but she would handle the situation all the same.

She slowed as she approached the ship and the encampment. She could see a line of girls chained up in the dark, and her expression twisted into something ugly and outraged. Before she could simply leap out of the trees and break the chain holding them in place, though, a Skaine rounded the ship. He was heading toward a row of bushes.

Well, Nickie had already known it was going to be a violent encounter. That was the entire reason they had come. She crept closer to the bushes, drawing her knife as she did. She paused for a moment a few yards from the tree line.

Perfect.

Rebus Quadrant, Regleon System, Swapayama

One Skaine's bladder could only hold so much. Gern staggered away from the table that had been hastily set up for dinner, and the only surprise was that he didn't piss himself as he stumbled past the bonfire. Only a few charred pieces of broken furniture were still recognizable in the flames.

He rounded the ship, and one of the girls immediately began praying under her breath when she saw him. Gern kicked a rock in her direction and found the closest bush.

Before he relieved himself, though, he paused. Someone was in the woods, heading right toward the ship. Gern squinted into the trees. "Belk, if this is you trying to be funny, you're doing a really bad job."

Whoever it was, it definitely wasn't Belk. Gern saw red eyes flash in the darkness, and he started backing away. He didn't make it more than a few steps before the red-eyed she-devil lunged out of the shadows. Gern had enough time to see the flash of firelight off her knife before the blade plunged beneath his chin. He had time for a single gurgling shout before she ripped the blade down, letting it follow the line of his throat until she split him from chin to sternum with a spray of blood.

Nickie wrenched the blade free, and the body dropped to the ground in a heap.

Gern had already shouted, though. And even when shit-faced and partying, Skaines were almost always on edge and ready for a fight. A moment later a few of them rounded the ship to see what was going on, and after that there was a mess of shouting, and soon what had to be every Skaine in the encampment was surrounding her.

Nickie grinned.

She was all right with that.

She flipped her knife to a reverse grip and spun, darting out of the way of a set of claws and sinking the blade to the hilt in the temple of the nearest Skaine. She ripped the blade free as the Skaine spasmed and dropped to the ground.

One down.

She dropped back into a backbend, back arching as she ducked under a barrage of laser fire. She turned it into a back handspring, kicking the Skaine trying to shoot her in the chin with enough force that she heard his vertebrae dislocate. Make that two.

She landed in a crouch, reached into her belt pouch, and threw her drones into the air. They whirred to life and broke off in three separate directions, ripping through Skaines like over-sized bullets. Nickie ignored them, content to let them do their thing without her input. Besides, she was a little bit busy.

She pulled her gun from its holster, pointed it to the side, and pulled the trigger. A Skaine dropped like a sack of rocks with a hole between his eyes, but Nickie had no time to appreciate the sight. A blast of laser fire came straight toward her, and although she twisted out of the way to avoid the worst of it, it still managed to graze her thigh. The smell of cloth and burning skin wasn't pleasant, and her expression twisted into almost comical outrage.

She rounded on the one who had shot her and threw her knife, and it sank straight into the Skaine's chest. He dropped backward, landing on two more Skaines behind him. Nickie took both of them out with her gun, then shot the one with her knife still sticking out of his chest for good measure.

She felt heat on her back as another laser blast ripped through her shirt, only narrowly avoiding raking a trench across her spine. She launched herself into a somersault over the three bodies in front of her, wrapping a hand around the hilt of her knife and pulling it free of the Skaine's chest as the somersault came to a standstill, leaving her crouched on all fours.

She dropped to a knee and pivoted, gun raised, and shot the Skaine who had tried to shoot her in the back between the eyes. But there was no time to celebrate. Another Skaine body-checked her, sending both of them tumbling to the ground in a heap. They grappled for a few drawn-out seconds before Nickie caught his head in both hands and cracked his neck sharply to the right. She kicked the body aside, only for another Skaine to lunge at her like a rabid mutt.

Blood sprayed out of the Skaine's chest as one of the drones ripped through it and sped on its way, painting Nickie like an ancient Pollock canvas. She rolled out of the way as the body toppled, and she dragged the back of one arm over her mouth. Mostly she just succeeded in smearing the blood across the bottom half of her face, but she could worry about that later. She got back to her feet and took a quick look around, assessing her situation.

Her drones were still doing their job like busily buzzing bees. Over half of the Skaines were dead.

Over half plus one a second later, as Nickie aimed her gun and fired and another one pitched to the ground with a hole through his guts.

There were steps approaching from behind her, and she could smell the plasma and ozone stink of a laser gun priming. She turned on her heel and lashed out, her fist meeting a Skaine's nose. With her other hand, she slammed her knife through his forearm, and he screamed as he dropped his gun on the ground. Nickie pulled her knife free with a bloody spray, flipped it over, and guided it upwards. It sank into the Skaine's chin, and he gurgled around the blade for a few seconds until Nickie pulled it out.

She kicked his body aside when it nearly landed on her shoes and took another quick look around, assessing and reassessing the situation to see how many Skaines were left. It didn't even occur to her to make sure that the girls hadn't been hurt or caught in the crossfire. She had barely even thought about them since her knife had cut the throat of that first Skaine.

There were few enough Skaines left that she could afford to take a few seconds and catch her breath. She watched her drones work. A Skaine tried to catch one of them, only for it to rip through his fingers like tissue paper. As he screamed over his shredded fingers, Nickie lifted her gun and put him out of his misery.

Of course, that only drew attention to her. Two more Skaines rushed her. She pirouetted out of the way of the initial charge and caught one of them by the back of his neck as he passed. With a grin, she tossed him into the air, and he flailed until all three drones found him. Like a pack of metallic piranha, they ripped him apart, blood falling like rain until the body hit the ground. Nickie fingered a loose strand of her hair distastefully. It was going to take her days to get all of it out of her hair, and she was probably going to look like a strawberry blonde for a week.

Her break had gone on long enough. She checked her gun and her knife with a cursory glance before looking around for the most convenient target. There were only a few left.

But she had let her guard down. There were only a few Skaines left, and her drones were so efficient. It seemed like she hardly had anything to worry about now—at least until one of the last Skaines, bigger than most of the others, even if that didn't mean much where Skaines were concerned, tackled her around the middle.

They hit the ground in a heap, scuffling as they fell. Nickie planted her foot against his chest and kicked him away, but he was on her again in an instant. She held him at bay with one of her knees, her shin against his chest and her knee just under his chin as he reached for her face with greedy, grasping claws. It looked like he wanted to rip her face off, and knowing what she did about the Skaines, that probably wasn't too far off the mark.

His claws came within a few millimeters of her nose before she kicked up and out, launching him over her head like a catapult. He hit the ground with a thump, and she could hear him scrabbling back to his feet. She had no plans to let him do anything else to her, though.

She rolled onto her stomach, stretched her gun out in front of her, and fired. The Skaine dropped to all fours as the shot ripped through one of his knees, and Nickie hopped back to her feet. With a deep breath, she kicked out, the heel of her boot slamming into his chin. His head snapped back with a crunch and a crack, and he toppled over backward. He didn't get back up.

Nickie lowered her leg until her boot was on the ground once more.

Chest heaving, she stood rigidly in the center of the

mess, glancing around with quick, sharp jerks. It took a few seconds for her to realize that she had run out of Skaines. She was standing in a field of bodies, with nothing left to fight. Moving like a wind-up doll that had been wound too far, she put her gun back into its holster and her knife back into her boot sheath.

She held a hand up and her drones returned like loyal retrievers, clinking together in her palm. She tucked them back into her belt pouch and gave it a pat, then finally turned to take a step toward the girls.

She froze in place before she could make her way over to them. They were all staring at her, all six of them, like they thought she was going to turn on them next. The youngest had started crying. They were covered in nearly as much blood as Nickie was.

With a jerk, Nickie took a step toward them, and they cringed and huddled together like cats in a storm. The youngest hid her face against the girl beside her, mumbling a steady stream of, "Please, please, please…"

"But—" Whatever Nickie was going to say never emerged, the rest of the words staying behind her teeth. Her expression went blank and she stepped forward, ignoring the way they cowered from her. She grabbed a length of the chain holding them and ripped it apart before moving on to the next length. Soon enough, the chain was lying in pieces on the ground.

The girls didn't thank her, simply stumbled to their feet and ran back toward their village as soon as they could. Nickie watched them go for a long moment, until their backs vanished in the darkness. Then she rounded on the Skaine ship, punching it hard enough that the metal dented inwards and one of her knuckles broke. She ignored the pain. Like the nearly healed laser blast on her leg, it would be fine soon enough.

She took off into the trees at a sprint. At that moment, she wanted to be on her ship and away from the entire planet.

Rebus Quadrant, Aboard the *Penitent Granddaughter,* Bridge

A trail of blood marked Nickie's path back through the ship and onto the bridge, in footprints and droplets that fell from her hair and her clothing and dripped off her chin. She really was coated. It was like she had decided to bathe in it.

Those girls were looking at me like I was a monster.

She dropped into the command chair. It was going to get filthy, and who knew what kinds of germs and diseases were in Skaine blood?

They were scared. They've been through a lot.

Nickie grunted in acknowledgment, but she didn't offer a response. Instead, she just stared at the main viewing screen as the ship took off once again. It didn't show anything unexpected, just the village and the grove of trees shrinking rapidly as the ship ascended.

It wasn't until the ship broke through the atmosphere and began building speed away from the colony that the door onto the bridge opened and Grim stepped into the room. Nickie had a very vivid recollection of the last conversation they'd had. Grim didn't look angry, though.

"You're filthy," he observed instead, coming to a halt beside her chair. "It's impressive."

"They took a few girls as…toys, I guess? I don't know." Nickie shrugged halfheartedly. "One of them was still a teenager. I set them free." She gestured as if that explained the mess perfectly. "None of those girls seemed impressed," she mumbled, picking half-dried blood out from beneath one of her thumbnails. "Based on how they looked at me, you'd think *I* was the monster."

Grim didn't say anything, and her thoughts kept churning until she offered quietly, "Maybe I am. I kind of feel like I might be."

Grim drew in a slow breath and sighed it out. "You're angry," he replied. "And you're hurt. Those things don't make you a monster."

Nickie nodded without looking at him, instead watching a drop of blood wind its way down the side of her boot until it reached the floor. Grim was apparently trying to put the words together to say something without saying it wrong, and Nickie was content to let him do the talking.

"You would have wound up in the same place no matter what," he said eventually, folding his arms over his chest. "The Skaines still would have attacked Themis and Swapayama, and you would still have fought them to stop them. Those Skaines would be dead regardless of what happened in the rest of the galaxy."

He was silent after that. Nickie finally slid him a side-long glance.

"The real difference is in you," he told her, gently but matter-of-factly. "If you're fighting because you have to—because it needs to happen and there's no other choice—it's a very different thing than fighting because you hate your target."

He gave her a moment to ponder his words, turning them over silently in her head and inspecting them from every angle. Once that moment passed, he told her, "Dinner's cooking. I figure you're hungry after today. I'll let you know when it's ready, but I'm not feeding you until you get cleaned up." He gave her a slightly pointed once-over before he turned and headed toward the door again, leaving her alone with that pearl of wisdom.

There was probably something she wanted to say about it, but in the end, it wasn't a conversation she needed to have with him. It was a conversation she needed to have with herself. He was happy enough to give her the tools to start it, but he wasn't going to hold her hand through it or have that conversation for her.

Alone with her thoughts, Nickie stared at the main viewing screen, watching space pass. It wasn't much to look at, but just then Nickie could appreciate the visual equivalent of white noise.

Hatred versus necessity.

But wasn't it all right to hate the Skaines? Didn't it make sense? They made hobbies and businesses out of murder and enslavement. What kind of person would she be if she *didn't* hate them? What kind of monster was she if she decided she was okay with it?

She dragged one hand through her hair, cringing slightly when her fingers got caught in a blood-coated tangle. She carefully worked them free as she emerged from her fugue state.

She didn't really understand any more now than she had a few hours ago. She just felt even more conflicted.

Hey, Meredith?

Yes?

I have no idea what my brain's doing or what I think or feel about any of this.

From what I know of human history and having access to the Archives, that seems to be the default state of humanity. I don't think it's cause for concern.

I guess not, but it means I need to figure it out.

One would assume so, yes.

Not really looking forward to that.

Those girls on Swapayama had looked at her as if she were a rabid wolf savaging their grandfather. Even as she had untied them, they had looked at her with naked fear.

She knew that she never wanted that to happen again. *She* never wanted to feel like that again, and a quieter part of her insisted she never wanted to make someone *else* feel like that again either.

She supposed that was at least a first step.

She took a breath and switched the main viewing screen to the rear cameras, watching Swapayama get smaller as they got farther away. It looked so quiet, but she knew what had happened there over the last few hours. Everything the Skaines had done.

Everything *she* had done, too, she supposed.

But all of that had already happened. At that moment, Swapayama was, at least for a moment, finally quiet.

She heaved a sigh, then got to her feet and headed for the door. Before the door could finish closing behind her, the bots were already cleaning up the mess she had tracked through the room.

Rebus Quadrant, Aboard the *Penitent Granddaughter*, Nickie's Quarters

As lacking as the luxuries on the former Skaine ship were, there was at least one definite perk to having taken over the captain's quarters—there was a bathroom attached. Granted, with only three people on the ship it wasn't much of a concern, but Nickie appreciated not having to worry about anyone else coming into the room as she washed blood out of her hair.

She kept her thoughts tracing along aimless paths. The way those girls had looked at her—like they couldn't tell her from the monsters under their beds—was still fresh in her mind. She kept her thoughts racing busily to avoid thinking back to them.

But what did *they* know? They didn't know what she had been through. They didn't know what it was like to have to fight like that. They didn't know *her*.

Their first impression of her had been that she was a monster. That she was just as scary as the Skaines who had snatched them away and chained them up.

She shook her head sharply as she pushed the thoughts away, spattering the walls of the shower with red droplets that soon got lost in the rest of the spray.

Her earlier guess had been correct. She sort of looked

like a strawberry blonde. She used the rest of her time in the shower grumbling about it incoherently as she lathered and rinsed her hair a fourth time.

She turned off the shower with a final surly, "Fucking iron, never going to rinse out." She wrapped a towel around herself and stepped out of the shower, fingering a strand of her hair as she did.

She left the bathroom and went back into her room, but her thoughts were still churning in circles. Even so, she at least felt less like she was some sort of muck monster.

Still wrapped in a towel and with her hair dripping down her back, she sprawled on her bed. It didn't matter if it got wet. She was still about fifty percent sure it was actually made of concrete and would dry again in no time.

She stretched her arms over her head before letting them go lax, fingers pressed to the wall behind the bed. She was half-asleep when Meredith interrupted her.

Now that everything is quiet again, it seems like a good opportunity to mention that another of your aunt's diary entries has unlocked. Would you like to read it?

Nickie took a breath, drawing herself out of her daze, and she sat up just enough to fold her arms under her head. Maybe Tabitha would tell her something that could help her wrap her thoughts around everything racing through her head. Her aunt could at least distract her for a little while.

CHAPTER 11 TABITHA

Planet Flex, Outside City of Karkat

"We are setting down outside Karkat," Achronyx announced. "If any further missiles are launched, they should be unable to reach us, and we can easily respond if necessary without harming civilians."

"Good," Tabitha replied. "Ryu, get ready. We're going into town."

She trotted off to her room to retrieve her favorite toys from her personal armory. It had been made to look like a jewelry case in an upscale closet. Black drawers slid out automatically, lit to show every weapon inside.

Achronyx's voice came over the speaker system. Tabitha was busy humming the tune to *Rawhide*. "Ranger Tabitha, I have some concerns about the addition to the bounty."

"You and Ryu should go talk about that, so you don't keep bothering me." Tabitha selected the little wand that would read a suspect's genetic code and match it to any known information on her end. She slipped it into one pocket of her jacket.

"My concern is not strategic. Eighty-five thousand credits is a considerable sum of money. Where do we propose to get it?"

"Oh, now I see what you mean." Tabitha chewed on her lip, remembering Bethany Anne's call. "Well, the way I see it, you don't have to pay assassins. It's blood money. That's beyond the rules of etiquette."

"The system required a deposit to post the offer."

"You should get that back."

"I anticipate that it will be difficult."

"*Psht.* Banking systems are easy." Tabitha blew a raspberry at the nearest speaker. "But if you really don't think you can do it, I'll handle that, and *you* go into town with Ryu to take out our targets."

The EI's voice was monotone. "I suppose you are making a joke of some sort?"

"Damn, you two are a tough crowd." Tabitha took out a pair of climbing gloves and slipped them into her pockets, then selected three of the pick-activated target-lock bombs. Almost as flat as paper, they were stickers that she could affix to a surface and activate for targeting.

She decided she probably didn't need more than three of them. "That would be a bad omen for the mission," she muttered.

"I will attempt to retrieve the money, then, so that we are not on the hook for the rest."

"Hey, wait a second!" Tabitha glared at the speaker. "That would mean I was dead! You're planning for if I die! That is not very supportive."

She left the room in a huff and met Ryu near the Pod bay.

"Problem?" he asked mildly, her eyes flashing red.

"Damn skippy, there's a problem. Achronyx is talking about where we'll get the money for the bounty, like we're going to die! And don't say you told me this was a risk. I don't want to hear it." She strode over to one corner of the Pod bay and pushed a button.

The lights came on over two motorcycles—or rather, antigrav bikes with flaring at both ends that looked almost like wheel-hubs.

"Let's go for a ride," Tabitha suggested happily.

"So these are the antigrav bikes. I wondered what they looked like."

"Just like Star Wars," Tabitha explained, in satisfaction. "Except aerodynamic. I guess Bobcat had some concerns."

She waited as the Pod bay door came down, then shot off toward Karkat with Ryu behind her.

City of Karkat, West Bar Side

"Okay, what are we looking for, exactly?" Ryu frowned. "I assumed you have found Walce, but Achronyx said—"

"We haven't found Walce." Tabitha looked at him, enjoying the way her ponytail swished behind her. "*Yet*," she added, a finger in the air. "But we will. We just have to get some information first."

"We should probably have changed, Kemosabe. I don't think, after what happened in the lounge, that people will be too eager to speak to us. Well, any of the people who could be useful."

"Don't be so negative."

"The people who run similar lounges will not be eager to see us arrive in case we do the same thing to their establishments, and the government officials won't look too kindly on the whole mess either."

"Funny you should mention government officials…"

"Oh, no." Ryu shook his head.

"You're completely right." Tabitha patted his arm. "You're an abomination that's half Ryu and half Hirotoshi, but you're also right—no one is going to want to talk to us. So we aren't going to try to talk to anyone."

"What's your plan? Let them come to us?"

"You'll see. Achronyx, any luck yet?"

Yes. Several bars meet your specifications. One is three blocks north. I will let you know which it is when you approach. The sign is in hieroglyphs I cannot read.

"What specifications did you give, exactly?" Ryu looked a little nervous. "Kemosabe…"

"Oh, don't worry so much. I just asked Achronyx to find me a bar that was *close* to government offices." She looked down at her shirt and gave a pleased smile. "You know, I might have been wrong about this one. It makes everything look so bouncy! If only they didn't still hurt," she groused.

"You healed from that almost immediately. There are no bruises remaining. Any pain is in your—"

Tabitha interrupted him. "Soul, yes. That someone could be evil enough to shoot something so beautiful as my rack." She looked at him. "Hirotoshi—"

"Ryu."

"We'll just see about that. As I was *saying*, it pains me deeply that someone could see such beauty and want to destroy it. Flex is truly a collection of the lowest of every species."

"No argument on *that* front. The level of corruption on this planet is insane. I'm surprised Bethany Anne hasn't simply told us to burn everything to the ground and start over. There are probably three or four worthwhile businesses, and maybe a dozen people who aren't aligned with some sort of mob."

Tabitha snickered. "Too true. Achronyx, is that it?" She pointed ahead at a building painted bright yellow. "The glow-in-the-dark one?"

If it is diagonally across the intersection from you, then yes. Additionally, please refrain from getting hit by the bus.

"What bus—"

Tabitha got hauled back onto the curb by Ryu as a double-wide three-story bus rattled past. It was a hovercraft in theory, but it looked as if it had maybe a half a street left before it fell apart. It was sagging toward the ground and shook as people left their seats to get to the exits.

"My guess," Ryu mused as he stared after it, "is that some of the money apportioned to public transit may have mysteriously gone missing. Just a guess, mind you."

"Hookers and blow," Tabitha agreed. "It's the same everywhere you go. Travel the universe, they said. See new places, they said." She headed across the street, bitching.

Ryu sighed and hurried after her. What had he been thinking when he put himself forward for this job? Things were much more fun when Hirotoshi kept Tabitha focused on the mission so Ryu could just worry about making well-timed quips.

Speaking of which, Hirotoshi would probably have gotten out of her what she was hoping to do in this club. Ryu hurried across the street to catch up with her.

"So, what is the game plan when we get inside?"

"Ah." Tabitha smiled. "We're going to find a private booth, then you're going to live it up like you're someone who knows how to have fun. I wouldn't worry so much, but...you know, you went through the transporter wrong and got turned into Hirotoshi."

"That poor man. Does he put up with this many insults on every mission the two of you do?"

"You already know." Tabitha sniffed. "You're him. You aren't going to throw me off with clever questions."

Ryu threw his hands up as they strode into the club. The bouncers hadn't stopped them, and he personally thought that was a very bad sign. A hundred-thousand-credit hit was out on them, and the bouncers were just letting them through?

"Kemosabe, what are *you* planning to do while I 'live it up?'"

"Let's get some drinks, and I'll explain." Tabitha waved at a waiter and gestured to herself and Ryu before giving an exaggerated shrug.

The waiter nodded. The request was common. With so many species around, it was easier to have a bartender simply mix something appropriate than it was to guess what might or might not kill a given race.

"That booth," Tabitha suggested, and they headed over to it and sat.

"So, what are we—" he asked before she cut him off.

She looked around, her voice a bit lower than normal as she scoped out the individuals. "Not yet. I'll explain."

Ryu sat praying for patience until their drinks arrived. He took a long pull of his and nodded. It was surprisingly good—fruity and sweet, reminding him a bit of a pina colada.

There were worse things in this world. It wouldn't do to look like he was enjoying it *too* much, though, or Tabitha would never stop giving him shit about it.

He looked at her...and his jaw dropped.

She was gone.

He hadn't even heard her move. She had just disappeared completely.

"Kemosabe?" He looked around the bar, lips pressed together. "Tabitha?"

"So, long story." Her voice came through his earpiece. "I'll be back shortly."

"Tabitha!"

"You sound like my mother right now. And an awful lot like Hirotoshi. What made you decide to swap faces? Neither of you is good-enough looking to want to engage in experimental procedures just to get that face."

Ryu sat fuming in the booth. He took a long pull of his drink.

"Ryu-toshi?"

"I'm subsuming my rage toward you in fruity drinks, and *what* did you call me?"

"It's my new name for you. Ryu-toshi and Hiro-u."

His eyes rolled to the ceiling - "That is entirely nonsensical, and if you translate—"

Tabitha spoke over his reply. "I'm a little busy right now. Live it up! I'll be back."

"Oh, I'll live it up. I'll live it up so much Bethany Anne will be calling to ask why you spent so much on bottle service. I'll live it up so much that— Kemosabe? Are you still listening?"

No answer. Ryu finished his drink and stared at the glass speculatively.

It was nearly impossible for a vampire to get drunk. He'd watched other people try and only shook his head. Right now, though, seemed like the perfect time to try. If he was a decoy, making a big show of living it up, there was going to be almost nothing equal to him downing enough liquor to get well and truly drunk.

He cracked his neck and stretched his fingers, then held up one hand.

"Waiter. Yes, hello. I would like forty-eight shots of the strongest liquor suitable for humans. After that, as soon as possible, please bring..."

A few floors up, Tabitha stifled her laugh as she eased herself through one of the windows and gripped the top of the window frame. The building actually got wider as it went up, so at this level, she was quite close to the government building next door.

She took a small grappling hook out of her coat and attached one end to her belt and the hook to the window. She hung for a moment before swinging herself sideways onto a small ledge, where she released the grappling hook and then flung it up into the darkness again.

She climbed up the wall, braced against the rope, and darted lightly across the tops of a few windows.

She was now close enough to leap to the government building. She landed on a windowsill and crawled into the shadow of a small deck, which she worked her way along the bottom of before poking her head over the edge to look.

No one was here. She used the railing to pull herself up and shook her head. Who put a natural climbing aid on the wall of a secure building?

Maybe aliens never did parkour.

Her target was in the top few floors of the building near the back. Tabitha used the deck's railing to get to the next floor, then found enough simple holds in the windows and wall materials to get up to the roof. She climbed over the railing and returned the grappling hook to her coat before checking her hair, tugging her shirt down, and heading for the door into the building with a smile.

She would have liked to have arrived on a helicopter, but a girl couldn't have everything. Besides, it would probably play havoc with her hair.

Inside the building, she headed down the stairs, freezing the security feeds as she went. During the day it would be too risky to do something like this. But at night in a back stairwell? No one could tell the difference between a still shot and a live feed.

Floor 18, Achronyx?

Yes. It's empty at present.

Thanks, Spanks.

Is that some human term I am unaware of?

No, I just made it up. Tabitha grinned as she trotted down the hallway. *I like it as a nickname for you, though. "Spanks." I think I'll keep using it.*

Is Spanx not a type of undergarment?

I wouldn't know. I never wear undergarments.

Have I mentioned how delightful I find it that we are more friendly with one another and able to share such confidences now, Ranger Tabitha?

Are you serious? Tabitha would not put it past Achronyx to say something like that and mean it, especially since he lacked any real context about undergarments. On the other hand, he did like to mock her.

Of course.

Well, that didn't clear anything up. She frowned as she laid a portable keypad over the electronic lock. It sensed the residual oils on the keys and began pressing buttons on its own, with pulses of a neuro-negative something-or-other EMP type release (shit that she tried to learn but finally gave up) in between to keep the lock from sending a distress signal at each failed login.

It found the correct code soon, and the door clicked open.

"Gotcha!"

Tabitha slipped inside and gave a pleased smile. The terminal here was exactly the sort of thing she was looking for: flanked by multiple monitors, each with a real-time feed of information, and a well-worn seat for some sort of alien who had a much bigger ass than she did.

I hope the head of security is a Flexxent, she sent to Achronyx. *Because if they're more bootylicious than me, I'm going to have to do something about it.*

Out of curiosity, what would you do?

I haven't decided yet. She sat in the large chair and began to work. The protocols were sophisticated, but she had seen better ones. You could only break into so many banks before most systems got boring. *Maybe I'd cut their ass off.*

I trust that is a joke.

Maybe.

She tapped a few keys. It seemed to be a universal fact that government security systems didn't use state-of-the-art technology.

"All right," she muttered, she looked up, down and all over the screen. "It has to be here somewhere."

Who was the bastard who had put a hit out on her? She was willing to bet that the government was monitoring things like that. Of course, they might be paid to turn a blind eye, but they'd certainly know about them.

It didn't take long to find the section relating to grey- and black-market transactions, but once she was there, she realized how much easier this would have been if it was legal.

The legitimate part of the market was much, much smaller in Karkat.

She gave a little sigh and kept searching. She was used to finding different querying methods and slipping her way through indexing systems in multiple ways.

Finally, she got a hit—on an abominable misspelling of her name that she was never, ever going to let the Tontos see. They'd tell Barnabas, and he would make it her nickname until one of them died.

Probably Ryu. Because she'd kill him.

The person who took out the hit was indicated in the government files simply as BSG.

Achronyx, any ideas who BSG is?

I'm still trying to figure out if my translation protocols are accurate. May I say, Ranger Tabitha, that spelling of your name is—

Something I had better not hear from anyone other than the two of us, Tabitha interrupted. *Understood?*

Of course, Ranger Tabitha. There was a whirring noise on Achronyx's end, and Tabitha decided to do some more digging for this BSG person. Might Benet Aljun'ra have another surname she was unaware of?

It is worth noting, Achronyx told her, *that in the bulletin that is out, the name of the client is not specified. Only here. Perhaps it is their equivalent of "John Doe."*

How many others have the same designation?

Fourteen.

I hope that's John Doe because otherwise this person collects hits like they're Pokémon. Tabitha kept typing, narrowing her eyes in thought. Where else to search? *Oh, this is interesting.*

What is?

I'll tell you when we're out.

Uh-oh, Achronyx said.

Uh-oh, what?

I found BSG. Or, should I say, the Bureau of Global Security. They put their modifiers before the nouns.

I don't care where they put their words! Are you telling me this is a government entity?

Yes. It appears to be their version of black ops.

Shiiiiit. Tabitha doubled down. Her work now had much more focus. She needed to get into these systems, get a lock in that she could hopefully keep accessing, and then get herself out of this building.

Achronyx let her work in silence for a few minutes, then said, *I estimate that you should leave soon, Ranger Tabitha.*

I know. Tabitha exited out of the computer system as quickly as she could, leaving it on the arrangement of screens that had been there when she arrived, and hurried back to the stairwell and then out to the roof.

She was climbing onto the side wall of the building when Achronyx reported, *It looks as though they have put out a more official bulletin for your arrest.*

More official? Tabitha lowered herself down the wall, clinging to it with her fingertips. *Sonofabitch, this hurts. Thank God I can grow my nails back super quickly.*

The hit on you is noted as BSG, which suggests the police may know that they are not to interfere. However, they seem to want to bring you in as well. I am not certain if this is an attempt to aid their black ops team.

Like hell am I going to spend any time in a police station on this visit.

May I point out that you pretty much entirely destroyed an upscale restaurant?

Nope. Tabitha leapt between the buildings again and scrabbled for purchase. For once, it was good that no one was there to see her. Cursing, she lowered herself back through the window and went down to check on Ryutoshi.

"What the hell?" He wasn't at the table, which worried her.

Achronyx, where is— Oh, my God.

Yes?

Um. Tabitha had no idea what to say to the vision in

front of her. *Things have gotten weird. Ryu is definitely not Hirotoshi, but I'm not sure who he* is.

There, in the middle of the club, Ryu was dancing as though he didn't have a care in the world. Surrounded by aliens, he was doing a very good imitation of whatever dance the others were engaged in.

The song ended, a new song started, and everyone gave a huge cheer—Ryu included. He threw his hands up and started into a complicated dance entirely on his own, and the rest of the aliens followed his lead.

Tabitha's mouth was hanging open.

Achronyx, are you seeing this? Tabitha turned back to look at the now empty booth where she had left him earlier. Then shook her head as she turned back to the person who looked eerily similar to Ryu, but was *dancing*.

Yes. I am not certain what is confusing to you. Ryu is a highly trained warrior. As such, it is not unlikely that he would be able to dance skillfully.

Oh, yes it is, Tabitha muttered. She pushed her way through the crowd to Ryu's side.

Ryu finally caught sight of her and gave a grin, taking his body through a series of moves that seemed to reverberate through him. "I'm living it up!" he waved to her. "Come on, dance!"

Tabitha looked around and tried to copy the moves, and it wasn't long before she was getting the hang of the footwork. "*Damn*, my ass looks fine when I shake it like this!"

"You can't see your ass!" he pointed out.

Tabitha snickered "I have a mental image, and it's *great!*" She put her arms up and twirled. "Oh, shit!"

"Oh, shit *what?*"

"Cops!" Tabitha hadn't seen Karkat's police force before, but she'd found that most cops looked pretty much the same—and there were three pushing their way through the crowd. There were indignant yells from the other dancers, and Tabitha jerked her head to the stairs in the back corner. "Come on!"

Ryu followed her, complaining all the way: "But I only just got them to bring me alcohol quickly enough for me to stay drunk!" He came around a corner too hard and slammed into the railing. "Damn!" This is *fun.*

"Just my luck that I'd have a drunk Tonto right now," Tabitha grumbled, "and not when I can take a holo and send it to Bethany Anne."

Ryu gave her a betrayed look. "You wouldn't. *Wait!*" He threw his arm out as they burst onto the roof. "Something about last time and roofs. We forgot something."

"To hit the right building?"

"No, that wasn't it." He swayed slightly, then snapped his fingers and made a jaunty dance move. "That's it! We forgot our harnesses."

Tabitha rolled her eyes. "Come on, drunk boy, jump!"

They pulled the tabs on their harnesses and went off the edge of the building, floating down gently.

"You *did* forget last time, though," Ryu insisted with the excessive seriousness of the gravely drunk. He hiccupped. "It's already fading."

"You're a Nacht. It was already gone." Tabitha rolled her eyes. "Come on, let's find a place to ditch our stuff and change, and then we can go somewhere for me to show you what I found in the computers. Oh, by the way, the hit on us is from Karkat's black ops."

"Why?" Ryu asked as they touched the ground.

"Hell if I know, but I am *damned* interested to find out." She headed into the crowd and pulled him along behind her. "Stay close. When I let you go off on your own, you start dancing."

City of Karkat, Six-Story-Tall Run-down Hotel

Tabitha looked around with a sniff and finally sat on the floor with a shake of her head. "This is terrible."

"I would think you have crashed in far worse places than this." Ryu raised his eyebrows as he lounged back on the couch. "It's soft. That's mostly what I care about. And before you mention diseases, remember we can't get sick."

"That we *know* of," Tabitha argued. "Maybe we can. Maybe this place has alien bugs."

"Of course."

"Germs." She eyed him.

"Herpes."

Ryu rolled his eyes, but Tabitha noticed he sat up and made sure not to touch the couch with his bare hands.

"And, yeah, I've crashed on a lot of people's couches, but that wasn't because I *wanted* to," she pointed out. "I'm not looking back on that time fondly or anything."

"It's not like you really have to stay here. We can probably leave in…how long, would you say?"

"I hope it's soon. I want Achronyx to have a look at this data." Tabitha waved the data stick. "Figures. I bust ass breaking into a government office, I get *good* stuff—oh, it's so good—and then I can't even go to the ship and revel in it." She looked around. "But I'm stuck here!"

"We should go to clubs more often." Ryu worked his shoulders. "That was *fun*. All you had to do was dance and yell, and everyone got happy. It's a simple life," he stated mock-wistfully.

"You forget how much alcohol it takes to make that fun night after night." Tabitha smirked. "Speaking of which, I saw that bill, and *you're* taking the next call from Bethany Anne about our expenses."

Tabitha was joking to calm her nerves. The fact was, what she had found made it very clear why the police were after them. They'd seen police searching through the crowds behind them long after she thought they'd give up, too, and now they were stuck here without the rest of her team, and without being able to have Achronyx crunch the data.

Ryu must have noticed. "So, what did you find?" He leaned forward on the couch. "Also, how do you think sitting on the floor is *safer*?"

"Have you considered what people do on that couch?" Tabitha asked him, one eyebrow raised.

Ryu looked down, a small look of disgust on his face as he stood up and came to sit with her on the floor.

"So, Etoy Walce," Tabitha began, snickering at Ryu's expression. "He's a criminal. We knew that. He's stealing all sorts of stuff, and just killing the people who have it so they won't make a fuss. Well, he's also one of their *government* agents."

Ryu whistled.

That's what you were going to tell me later? Achronyx asked.

"Yep," Tabitha told him. Since Achronyx could hear her either way, she preferred to speak out loud when she didn't have to be quiet.

"So is that why the police were after us?" Ryu asked. "I figured it was just because of the lounge."

"I thought so, too, but I'm beginning to wonder. They tailed us for a really long time." Tabitha frowned. "Here's the thing… That hit on us was put out by their government black ops group."

Ryu whistled once more. He caught himself slouching and sat up straight the way Hirotoshi would have, and Tabitha gave him a look, raising an eyebrow like Bethany Anne would. *Two can play this game!*

"Continuing with your weird-ass impersonation?"

"I am *trying* to bring a little dignity to this mission," Ryu corrected loftily.

Tabitha smiled, but he noted she looked a little bit worried. "If we had done more research on Walce before coming in, we might have figured out that he was a government agent as well as a criminal."

"Is he really a criminal if he works for them?" Ryu asked philosophically.

"I don't think he steals things *for* them, he just also does that… Or, wait—are you suggesting that Karkat is poaching building supplies and food from other planets? That would be *cold*."

"It can't be the first time it's happened, though. Human countries used to encourage piracy against one another's ships. Why pay for supplies for their civilians when they could just steal them?"

"That makes sense." Tabitha considered. "We should get some rest. We'll head back as soon as Achronyx says the coast is clear."

I'll keep watch, Achronyx told them. *Right now, there are still police canvassing the area. They already came to this building but were told that there was no one matching your description.*

"Yeah." Tabitha grinned. "I told them I was Ryu's mistress, and he'd pay a lot to make sure his wife couldn't find me. I said she was some government bigwig. Look at how this hotel is kept up! They aren't going to like the police."

"You said you were my what?" Ryu asked plaintively.

She eyed him. "Don't look so insulted. The receptionist was only surprised you hadn't put a ring on my finger to lock *this* down." Tabitha smacked her ass, somewhat impeded by the fact that she was sitting on the floor.

Ryu grumbled, but he pulled his coat off and used it as a pillow so he could drift off to sleep.

Tabitha did the same, but she frowned up at the ceiling as she drifted off. Twice now she had underestimated Etoy Walce. She had gone to the government building expecting to find a dossier that would lead her to some of his hiding places. He *was* a well-known criminal, after all.

Instead, she'd gotten tangled up in something larger than she'd expected.

She should have brought the rest of the team. She

crossed her arms over her chest, gave a pleased grin, and fell asleep.

The police patrols have withdrawn to specific points in the city to keep watch, Achronyx reported a few hours later. *I have charted a path for you that will take you through the dead zones in their surveillance.*

"I'm up," Tabitha muttered, picking her head up and squinting. "Mostly." She stood up with a groan and shook herself out. One thing that didn't change when you became a vampire was that pins and needles still knocked you for a loop. She flapped her arm, annoyed. "This is a pain in the ass."

"And you look ridiculous," Ryu added.

"Thanks. I can't tell you how nice it is to have the support of my team. Achronyx, are they watching the ship?"

No, they seem to think you'll stay in the city.

"Their loss. Come on." Tabitha led Ryu out the window. "I got this place for the week, so they won't come looking for us for a *while.*"

"We'd come out every so often anyway, right?"

"They think we're going at it like rabbits. They're not going to walk in there."

Ryu gave a pained look.

They went to the edge of town and retrieved their bikes, heading quickly and quietly into the darkness.

City of Karkat, Outskirts, QBS *Achronyx*

Tabitha pulled her antigrav bike into the Pod bay of the *Achronyx* and turned it sideways to skid to a stop. She had thought the effect would be a little less amazing without squealing tires, but she wanted to swish her ponytail dramatically.

Not only did the ponytail-swish go exactly according to plan, but it also turned out that skidding sideways to a stop on an antigrav bike was even cooler than one on tires.

"Aw, hell yeah." She swung her leg over the bike and struck a pose. "Mama *likes* these. Great for finding guys to add to my list."

"You and your list," Ryu grumbled as he pulled his bike neatly into position and dismounted. "Are you going to park properly?"

"Why are you so boring?" Tabitha groused, but she got back on the bike and pulled it alongside his. "There. Is that good enough for you, Ryu-toshi?"

Ryu just shook his head as they walked toward the bridge.

"Welcome back, Ranger Tabitha," Achronyx said. "I have news for you regarding the bounty for your death. It has been increased."

"I know. No one's gonna put a lousy fifteen-thousand-credit hit on *me*. Achronyx, can you tell if anyone actually *interesting* is on the job now?"

"You're insane." Ryu shook his head, annoyed. "Your ego and pride are *way* bigger than your bodaciousness."

Tabitha stopped dead, looking at him. "You take that back!"

"Never," Ryu retorted. "You might end up paying for your own hitman!"

"What I was referring to," Achronyx raised his voice above theirs, "is that the original group has increased the bounty. The total now stands at a hundred and eighty-five thousand credits."

Tabitha whistled. "Now *that's* some good shit. They're all gonna be coming after this." She looked down at her armor with a self-satisfied grin. "And I'm gonna look fine as hell while I show each and every one of those fish-fucking, dick-headed, no-balled sphincter-brains what it means to fuck with a Ranger." She gave Ryu a grin.

He looked at her, his eyes blinking with no emotion on his face. "You're not at all upset, are you?"

"I'm *going* to kill whoever decided to put the hit out on me," Tabitha assured him as if this solved everything. "I just didn't want it to be open mic night at the hit-club. I want the pros." She shrugged off her coat and slid sideways into the captain's chair, draping herself over it with a grin. "Achronyx, find out who *specifically* is running the bounty, and I'll add his name to the list of people whose ass I plan to kick."

"Yes, Ranger Tabitha." Achronyx's voice was bland.

Ryu gave a look at the speakers and shook his head. He knew that Achronyx was often sarcastic, but sometimes it was genuinely hard to tell if the EI knew how ridiculous Tabitha was being.

Still draped over the chair, head hanging upside down, Tabitha held up a memory stick with a flourish.

"This is the information I got on their computers," she announced. "Ryu, would you plug it in? I want to have Achronyx take a look at it."

With a good-natured sigh, Ryu stood up and retrieved

the stick. He plugged it in, and Achronyx began to bring the files up on the main screen. Tabitha sat up to watch, curling her legs under her and narrowing her eyes every once in a while.

After a few minutes, having sorted the information Tabitha found into relevant groups, Achronyx told them, "There is much interesting information here. Most likely, I will need several hours to do a thorough analysis."

"Anything interesting right *now?*" Tabitha pouted slightly. "I want to get back out there now."

"You should get some rest," Ryu advised. "Actual rest, on a bed that isn't coated with alien...stuff." He looked a little queasy.

Tabitha gave a full-body shudder. "We should probably take showers before we get any diseases."

"Agreed."

They both stood up, and Tabitha was starting to leave when she did a double-take at the screen. "Who's that?"

"Dev Zancred," Achronyx reported. The full dossier came up on the screen.

Tabitha strolled closer to look. "Hmm. Interesting. Oh, that's *very* interesting. I like that."

Ryu peered at the screen. "What, exactly, do you like? This man is a revolutionary. He provides help to groups who back all kinds of shady people."

"Bethany Anne is a revolutionary."

"Bethany Anne overthrows violent dictatorships. This man supports them."

"He's cute, though."

"He's...what?" Ryu's jaw dropped.

"Look, just because he has bad political leanings doesn't

mean I shouldn't be able to date him. Tack him onto my list, Achronyx."

"The list of individuals whose asses you plan on kicking?"

"No, you Intel Celeron Neanderthal, the ones I plan on overcoming with my skills and overwhelming attractions." Tabitha trailed her hands down her sides with a grin. "I'll show up and show *him* the time of his life, and he'll come to the light side of the Force. I promise. I can pull it off. I'm *that* good."

She strutted off, tapping her hip to a beat Ryu couldn't hear, and Ryu stared after her with a frown.

Ryu, Achronyx asked privately, *do you think she knows that he is part of a group who abstains from sex? Also, they are strictly focused on their own species. They ban members from mating with non-Torcellans. This male would not mate with a human.*

Can we confirm that Tabitha is even human? Ryu countered with a grin. *She could have been changed in the Pod-doc —just enough.*

He shook his head. After Shin's death, she had regressed back to a younger version of herself, not quite the Ranger she had been before. He and Hirotoshi had been working hard—hell all of the Tontos had been working hard—to help her pick up the pieces.

He just hoped she reconnected with the old Tabitha before she made one too many mistakes.

"I finally feel *human* again." Tabitha emerged from her room a few hours later, swishing her newly-clean hair back and forth. She was dressed in a pair of spotless black pants with a leather-and-wool top.

"I still think we should both take a turn in the Pod-doc," Ryu joked. "I took three showers, and I'm not sure I'm clean yet. How did they think we'd spend a week in that room without dying?"

"Alien herpes doesn't kill you, it just screws up your junk." Tabitha grinned. "It's incurable, and everybody knows what messed-up shit you've been doing."

"The badge of shame for your bits," Ryu joked.

"It's an achievement!"

"If you are both *quite* finished," Achronyx interrupted, "I have found multiple locations for you to investigate. Three, to be precise."

"None of them are grungy motels, right?" Tabitha asked as she sat cross-legged in one of the chairs. "Let's see 'em."

"The first location is of a Flexxent named Kenet Aljun'ra."

"Kenet Aljun'ra, Benet Aljun'ra…" Ryu frowned.

"They are siblings."

"Who are the rest of them?" Tabitha quipped. "Tenet, Menet, Wenet?"

"Wenet, Renet, and Flenet," Achronyx replied.

Tabitha and Ryu looked at one another.

"Are you messing with us?" Tabitha asked.

"I would never do that. In any case, it is my guess that after the incident at Benet's lounge, Kenet became aware of your presence on the planet."

"Wait a sec." Ryu took a sip of his coffee and frowned.

"Are you suggesting that because we smashed up Benet's lounge, the Karkat black ops team has it in for us? Or is it just a wild abuse of power on Kenet's part?"

"It is difficult to say at this time. Nevertheless, I have conclusively traced the origin of the hit to him. He can be found here in Karkat, in one of the mansions in the city's gated district."

"Schmancy," Tabitha mocked. "Wonder how he'll get when he realizes gates don't keep people out?"

"Bet he runs," Ryu suggested wickedly.

"Bet he cries."

Ryu sniffed. "Obviously."

"The *second* location," Achronyx said, struggling to keep them on task, "is that of Grule Jino'sha, a well-known Flexxent assassin who seems to be tracking Tabitha. I received word of his interest in the case. I believe he is waiting at this location near where Tabitha was last seen."

Tabitha nodded.

"And this," Achronyx continued, "is the third location. Ranger Tabitha, this is the home of Dev Zancred."

"Ooooh."

Why are you giving her the location of a revolutionary she wants to bone? Ryu asked Achronyx.

I should think it was obvious, the EI replied. *To make things interesting.*

Ryu grumbled internally.

"Achronyx, you keep an eye on Dev," Tabitha directed. She grinned at the screen and made a kissy face. "I'm coming for you, baby. *Yes,* that was a double entendre. *Damn,* I'm good. Just gotta take out that assassin first."

Ryu relaxed slightly. "Yes, I agree. We don't want to get

close to taking Kenet out, only to have an assassin suddenly in the mix."

"Exactly." Tabitha headed for the door. "Let's go into town and get all these annoying bastards out of our hair. Then I can seduce the revolutionary and—"

"Kemosabe, what about Etoy Walce?"

She threw a hand up in the air, annoyed. "*Gott Verdammt!* I'd forgotten about him."

Ryu rolled his eyes and followed her from the room.

City of Karkat

The antigrav bike ride back to town was pleasant. It was a beautiful fall day—or, at least, from the weather it would have been a beautiful fall day on Earth, with the sun shining and a brisk breeze as the antigrav bikes cut through the landscape.

Karkat came up quickly in their view. Most of the planet wasn't occupied, so the main city had simply taken the same name. A bit confusing sometimes for planning hits, but rarely misleading.

"Our first target is close to the center of town," Ryu told Tabitha. "Achronyx says he hasn't moved far."

They slowed down and stowed their bikes in an abandoned building, making sure to pick a different one from before. Tabitha had learned back when she was fending for herself not to let patterns help people find her. You didn't park in the same place every time, sneak into a building the same way every time, or even go into a computer system the same way every time.

That was how you got caught. And then dead.

She adjusted her coat as they walked, making sure to look all around her as if she were a tourist, not a trained killer.

Sometimes it was useful to be five foot four. When John Grimes walked into a room, everyone knew to be afraid—well, the armor usually helped with that impression—but when Tabitha showed up, many people didn't know to take her seriously.

She had fun disabusing them of that notion.

As they passed one of the first major streets, there was a flash out of the corner of her vision. Both she and Ryu looked over more quickly than any non-vampire could.

There was nothing there anymore, but both of them were instantly on guard.

"Achronyx, let us know if anyone is sneaking up on us."

"I will do so, Ranger Tabitha."

Ryu nodded. Tabitha had spoken on the non-private channel. He wasn't sure what they had seen, but he knew that in a city like Karkat, where they already had a huge hit out on them, it wasn't likely to be an accident.

Grule got a notification from his personal alert system and downed his beer before looking at it. He hated humans, but he liked their beer.

Only good thing about them. Now that everyone knew how to make it, he figured he could kill every human he found. Based on what he'd seen, everything else they produced was just trouble.

When he saw the notification, he smiled. The two targets were on his radar and heading directly for him in the center of town.

He wondered if they knew about the hit out on them. They must not. After all, the bonus had been upped twice already. BSG was impatient on this one.

The Flexxent wasn't stupid. He knew just who had ordered the hit, even if they tried to hide it. He hadn't wanted any part of it when it was a paltry fifteen thousand credits, but a hundred and eighty-five thousand?

That was a job he could get behind.

He nodded to the bartender to put the drink on his tab, then headed to the back room he rented here. It wasn't where he lived, but he had rooms all over the city where he stashed weapons and armor.

He came out a few minutes later with a full suit of relatively light and unobtrusive armor. He'd paid a *lot* of money for it. It was absolutely top of the line. No one had anything better, he was sure.

Grule wouldn't live long enough to meet Jean Dukes, so he would be dead before ever learning that his armor was inferior.

He used the alley to get out of the building and climbed up to the roof on a retractable ladder he flung up ahead of him. There, he carefully took up position and waited. His targets would be in range soon. Two quick shots and they'd be dead.

Grule was no longer the only one searching for Tabitha, however. The two increases in the bounty had been noticed by a large number of people, and even some non-assassins were thinking they might join the fight.

"It's the perfect crime," Lore aleni'Tath told her fellow police officer. She leaned across the table and jabbed her finger on it for emphasis. "We're already supposed to be looking for her to arrest her, so we just head over there, it turns into a shootout, and she's dead. We get the bounty, and no one's gonna come down on us because they know she's violent."

"I don't know," the other Flexxent replied dubiously. Rino Wex'ra had made a career of doing everything by the book. He was pretty sure that if anyone else had been in the office today, Lore wouldn't be working with him.

But they were all still off manning their corners, looking for the human.

"Oh, come *on*, Rino." Lore crossed her arms. "You're so stubborn and unimaginative when you're male."

Rino shook his head. He was like this all the time, and she knew it. Flexxent tended to switch sexes every few months regardless of their choices in the matter, but could also change at other times if they were around another Flexxent giving off mating pheromones, and sometimes just if they wanted to.

With such an ability, there were extensive debates about whether an individual's personality changed with their sex. Aliens reported being entirely confused by the Flexxent's gender rules, some of which seemed to be very strict, others very lax. It all made complete sense to the Flexxent, but they were the only ones.

Rino generally preferred to be male. There wasn't anything in particular that bothered him about being female; he just preferred to be male. He really didn't think his personality changed, but he knew he wasn't going to convince Lore. Now that she had a point to prove in the conversation, she was going to keep arguing it no matter what.

And apparently, *he* was the stubborn one.

"Well," he agreed finally, "since we have to find her anyway, we might as well go."

"Exactly. And no one has to know she didn't shoot first."

"You're making an assumption," Rino cautioned.

"What?"

"That she *won't* shoot first."

He'd seen the security footage from the Yud Skrow Lounge. He didn't think it was a safe assumption that they could apprehend this woman without getting shot at. That was his job, though, and he was determined to do it.

He would decide about the rest when it went down.

Grule saw them as they came onto the main thoroughfare. It was just as the bulletin had described: two humans, one shorter than the other, one with dark hair, one with light, both with pale skin.

He had looked at the pictures, but he still couldn't tell the two of them apart. Human features just had no definition, and it was especially difficult in this case when they had the same coloring.

Humans didn't seem to have any interesting colors at all, actually. They were all browns and tans with a little bit of pink.

Beer. That was the only good thing humans had given

the universe. Everything else about them was insufferably frustrating.

He guessed that the shorter one was the female, but he planned to kill them both just in case. He didn't make a habit of leaving loose ends.

He aimed at the shorter one. It had gathered its hair in one area, which then fell down its back and swished, and it seemed to enjoy turning its head quickly to make the hair fly around in an arc. As Grule watched through his scope, it gave a little dance and tossed its hair at the other one.

This was a warrior fearsome enough that BSG was ordering its death?

Grule shook his head slightly and shrugged. It was their money.

He chambered his first round with a click, aimed, gently squeezed the trigger and shot.

In the street below, screams erupted. People ran for cover as dust billowed. Grule used explosive rounds. In this case, he might even have taken out her compatriot as well. He kept his attention focused, scanning back and forth while he waited for the dust to clear.

Finally, it settled on the empty street, and he leaned forward, smiling in anticipation. A nice, clean shot. Any moment now, he should be able to see the outline of a body. Hopefully, two. And blood. Did humans bleed green, or was that Torcellans?

Whatever the case, it was hard to mistake a puddle of blood for anything else.

He was so sure of what he was going to see that he was still staring at the street long after he should have realized the truth.

There were *no* bodies. The round appeared to have struck the paving stones since several of them had been reduced to stone chips and a few others had been tossed out of place by the explosion.

There was no way they could both have just coincidentally gotten out of the way of that shot, was there?

Then a faint sound reached his ears, and he leaned forward to look over the edge of the building. His heart caught in his throat.

The smaller human was climbing the wall, scaling what should be a smooth surface with ease. When it looked up at him, he saw its eyes were bright red.

And he couldn't see the other one at all. Grule stood and ran for his bag of weapons on the other side of the roof. A sniper rifle was clearly not going to do the trick anymore.

———

"Kemosabe, we should make a plan." Ryu used the Etheric comm as he ran around the back of the building. "I am going around to the back and will try to cut him off there. If he—"

"There's no need for a plan! He's cornered up there. He has nowhere to go. Anyway, I'll be up there soon." Tabitha grunted over her feral grin.

On her last visit to the *Meredith Reynolds,* she had gotten a set of gloves that gave her purchase even on the smoothest of surfaces. Little claws, too small to be seen by even her eyes, would hook into the wall she was climbing and retract as she lifted her hand to the next hold. Despite their tiny size, the hooks were strong enough to hold her.

She wondered if they would hold in the event of an explosion. She'd had a very unpleasant experience with that not too long ago.

She had heard the click as the Flexxent chambered his weapon, and she and Ryu dived in opposite directions, her forward and him back. By the time the smoke cleared, she was already a story or so off the ground on the wall of the building.

The Flexxent had seen her climbing. She hoped the fucker was wetting himself.

Just in case he had something to drop on her, she made her way along the wall and turned the corner. This building had extensive ornamentation on the sides, only really visible from the alleys.

Architects in Karkat were ridiculous.

It was a quicker climb when she had proper handholds. She stowed the gloves and shinnied up the wall, swinging and taking the time to do one loop-the-loop around a stone gargoyle that looked stable enough.

"I'm close to the roof," Ryu reported. "If I get his attention, you can come up over the roof and—"

"Ryu! For the last time, I've got this." Tabitha shook her head as she came up over the edge of the wall.

A few seconds later, a gigantic kinetic slug hit her in the chest and bowled her off the roof.

"SONOFA—" That hurt like unholy fuck. Tabitha grabbed for a gargoyle and missed. She hit another one, tumbled off it, and at last managed to grab at one as she went past, ending up gripping the statue like a sloth.

Her chest ached like a motherfucker. "Donkey-licking ape-tit twister," she moaned aloud. "I need a new ribcage."

———

Up on the roof, Ryu had watched Tabitha get blown backward. "Achronyx! Is Tabitha all right?"

"One moment. I am assessing the situation. She missed the first hold and the second hold. This reminds me of a pachinko machine. Ah, she's caught one now. She appears to be healing."

Satisfied that Tabitha did not need urgent medical care, Ryu charged the Flexxent while its back was turned. It was holding a gigantic gun, which seemed to be heavy enough that even the Flexxent's huge muscles were straining to hold it.

Perfect.

He hit it in the back of the knees and realized his mistake when the Flexxent collapsed on him. Ryu struggled to flip over and managed to turn enough to land a few punches, but Grule staggered up and started running for his bag of weapons.

"Oh, no, you don't!" Ryu yelled. He increased his speed in a burst few other species could match and leapt. One leg flicked out. It would have been a delicate motion, except for the fact that Ryu had spent centuries mastering his technique. He hit the alien like a locomotive. There is a certain mass with velocity even when gravity is lower.

The Flexxent went staggering, trying to get its bearings back after being hit so hard in the head.

"Kemosabe, are you recovered?"

"Guhhhhhhhh."

"It does not appear so, Ryu."

"Yes, I gathered that much. Thank you, Achronyx." Ryu rolled his eyes. He grabbed the Flexxent's bag and threw it over the edge of the roof, hoping it would get caught on one of the gargoyles for retrieval later.

He was *very* curious about some of its weapons.

"Kemosabe, I need some help." He spoke over their communications. "The Flexxent can absorb hits like you wouldn't believe."

Tabitha gave the mental equivalent of a gurgling noise, and that was when Grule stopped staggering around. His eyes turned and focused on Ryu.

Shit. Ryu managed to get out of the way as the Flexxent charged. It slammed its fist into the ground and skidded to stop itself, and the whole roof shook.

"You might want to work on your pull-back," he informed the alien.

Ryu ducked under another swing and managed to get a few hits in before dancing away again, but he was concerned. None of his hits seemed to be doing lasting damage to the Flexxent, and he was not sure how many he could take.

He ducked away from another swing and backed up as Grule advanced, roaring.

"I will end your miserable life, human!" Grule bellowed at him. "You and the other one. Tell me, which one is Ranger Two?"

"I am!" Ryu replied.

Tabitha sounded a bit muzzy. "Low Ryu, that's really low. I get knocked out once, and you take my spot."

"I'm trying to throw him off of the building Kemosabe." Ryu ducked away from a blow and managed to catch the Flexxent in the side of the head. He yelled in pain.

"Oh. That's very nice then."

"I don't suppose you're available to help." He really wasn't getting anywhere.

"Soon. I feel like I got kicked by a horse on steroids."

"I've seen the gun he used. You're lucky that's all it feels like." Ryu kicked at where a human would have kneecaps, but that didn't seem to do any good.

He couldn't avoid the next punch, and it caught him full in the torso. Ryu went over backward and skidded, groaning as he picked himself up. Tabitha's horse-kick analogy seemed accurate.

Apparently, however, Grule was not used to anyone getting up after he hit them. He stared at Ryu for a moment, his jaw hanging open, then ran to the edge of the building and jumped. A moment later he appeared in a small hovercraft, heading at high speed for the other side of the city.

Ryu swore. A few seconds later there was some scrabbling and Tabitha came over the edge of the roof.

"Where is he?"

"He got away." Ryu pointed to the east, disappointed.

"Where the hell did that coward go?" Tabitha demanded. "Ohhhh, he better not be running. Any hitman who tries to kill me and then runs away will get what's coming to him. Achronyx?"

"I tracked him to a small building on the edge of town," Achronyx reported. "I no longer read any heat signatures inside the building. My guess is that it leads to a series of tunnels. I will let you know when and if he emerges."

"Oh, I hate that," Tabitha fumed.

"We might have been able to take him if we had attacked at the same time," Ryu offered. "Without him having a chance to aim and fire, we could have overwhelmed him. He takes hits well, but with both of us working together, we would have won."

"Yeah, Flexxent are *tough*. Too bad we don't have one for practice on the *Meredith Reynolds*." She snickered and trotted off to examine the gun. "This thing is nice!"

"Kemosabe…" But Ryu knew from experience that when Tabitha was not yet ready to admit a mistake, he was not going to score any points in the conversation.

Hopefully, she would learn before this mission became an unmitigated disaster.

He was mentally reviewing the layout of the city, trying to figure out if they should attempt to get to Kenet before finding Grule, when there was the boom of a gun and Tabitha yelled angrily.

The blast had come from behind Tabitha, and it knocked her back. She tripped over the heavy gun and went sprawling. There was the smell of burning, and she just *knew* there was a smoking hole in the back of her jacket now.

She was on her feet the next moment, eyes flashing red as she turned to see a Torcellan assassin standing on the edge of the roof. His pale skin shone silvery-white in the sunlight and his hair was done up in a ridiculously ornate series of braids, several of which had flashing lights in them.

Torcellans. Even the assassins weren't practical about their hair.

"Didn't you hear, asswipe?" Tabitha yelled. "Shooting me in the back is now a punishable-by-death offense!"

The Torcellan, who had clearly not expected her body armor to absorb the hit, threw a tiny grappling hook out of his belt and began rappelling hastily back down the side of the building.

"He is so dead!" Tabitha sprinted for the edge of the roof.

"Let me kill him." Ryu was running as well. "Kemosabe, I apologize. I was lost in my own thoughts, and I did not hear him come up onto the roof—"

Not to be outdone, Achronyx added, "I must apologize as well. I was focused on surveillance footage of the city."

"We'll talk about this later!" Tabitha yelled at both of them. She drew one of her knives and skidded to the rope, slashing at it. Somewhere below, there was a scream—and a couple of seconds later, a dull thud.

Tabitha and Ryu jumped off the roof and activated their harnesses.

"But we have to talk about it now," Ryu argued as they floated down. "It's affecting our combat. It's critically, immediately important."

"No time!" Tabitha landed and rolled. The Torcellan was moaning on the ground, and she stalked over to him. "You. *Asswipe.* I suppose it would be too convenient for you to be Etoy Walce."

He looked at her wide-eyed. The fall seemed to have knocked the wind out of him enough that he couldn't speak or think properly.

Tabitha pulled her identification wand out of her jacket and knelt next to him, pressing one end against his skin. To her annoyance, it flashed red.

"Damn. That really would have salvaged this day, you know?" she bitched to Ryu. "We could have brought him back, thrown him in the brig, and then cleaned this whole city up."

He looked over his shoulder at the buildings nearby. "I think that would take a lifetime of work, Kemosabe."

"You're very negative these days, you know that, Ryu-toshi?" Tabitha knelt to glare at the Torcellan on the ground. "You. What do you know about Kenet Aljun'ra?"

The assassin looked panicked at that name. He struggled to sit up and seemed to be trying to bargain for his life, waving his hands at them pleadingly.

"Nuh-uh." Tabitha stood up, crossed her arms, and planted her foot on his chest. "No way. You failed to kill me, which means you answer my questions. And you tried to shoot me in the back, which means maybe I kill *you*."

"Maybe?" Ryu asked.

"Well, if I promise to kill him he has no incentive to answer me, does he?"

"Oh, I hadn't thought of that. Why wouldn't you just not mention it, then?"

"I didn't think it all the way through."

The EI's voice came over the comm. "I would agree with Ranger Tabitha on that point."

"Achronyx, you ass!"

The EI sat in smug silence and Tabitha fumed. He was very good at saying respectful things—or things that *sounded* respectful or *should* be respectful, but you could just tell weren't really.

"I'll get you for that," Tabitha promised him.

Ryu maintained an impressively straight face and tried with everything he had not to laugh. "So, what do we do with this one?"

He wasn't even finished with the last word before the Torcellan pulled out a hidden gun and tried to shoot them again. However, the Torcellan was still somewhat dazed from his fall, and Tabitha and Ryu both used their good reflexes to good effect. As soon as they saw the gun, both of them ducked.

Tabitha's eyes flashed again. She grabbed the Torcellan's arm and ripped the gun away before throwing him against the wall of the building.

"Listen, you useless ingrate!" A punch slammed the Torcellan's head against the wall, and he gave a moan of pain. "You have the fucking nerve to shoot me in the *back* —" Another punch punctuated this statement. "And now you try to shoot me when I am giving you a chance to live?" She punched him twice more, and added another punch for emphasis.

"You said you were going to kill me anyway!"

She stopped her punches. "I said I *might*. You'd have had better odds telling me about Kenet. What, do you work for him or something?"

"Everyone in Karkat works for him," the Torcellan whimpered. "You don't do anything here without his say-so. If I double-cross him I'll never work here again, and he'll put a hit out on *me*."

"Ask me how much I care. No, seriously, ask me."

Tabitha sighed as the assassin stayed quiet. "He's not going to ask me, is he?"

"I don't think so," Ryu told her.

"Okay, how about this?" Tabitha picked the Torcellan up and used his head to break a window. "Tell me what you know about him, and I won't do that again."

"Augh! I don't know much, I swear!" The Torcellan was babbling now. "He's Flexxent! Their family is rich! I don't know anything else!"

"Why does he want me dead?"

"I don't *know*!"

"Ugh." Tabitha rolled her eyes. "Fucking useless. All right, listen up. I am giving you *one chance.* I shouldn't even do that. I should just shoot you in the back and call it even, but I have a lot of people to track down, so consider this your lucky day."

She went through the Torcellan's clothes methodically, pulling out every weapon she could find and storing them in her pockets.

"I'll just take this, and this, aaaaand this. And that. Anything else? Hmm." She flipped him upside down and shook him by the ankles, him bitching the entire time, but nothing else came out. "I guess that was everything. Go find a new planet and a better career."

The Torcellan, now bleeding from his nose, landed hard in the dust, staggered up, and stumbled off with a panicked look over his shoulder.

"I think I'm growing as a person." Tabitha looked at Ryu. "Showing mercy, you know?"

Ryu watched the man duck around a corner and disappear before turning to Tabitha. "Are you *sure* hitmen were the place you wanted to start with that?"

"That's enough sass for now, Number One."

"For the last time, I am *not* Hirotoshi." Ryu gave an elegant bow. "That said, Kemosabe, perhaps we should proceed to the next point in our itinerary."

"This from the man who was throwing his hands up in the club and ordering bottle service last night. Yeah, that's right, I got the bill." Tabitha glared at him.

"You said to live it up," Ryu reminded her innocently.

"You knew what I meant. I meant—"

"I hate to interrupt, but perhaps you two should look behind you."

Tabitha and Ryu looked around.

"Aw, hell," Tabitha muttered. There, wearing what were clearly police uniforms, stood two officers with wicked-looking guns already drawn.

CHAPTER 14 TABITHA

City of Karkat

"I still don't think this is a good idea," Rino muttered as he and Lore moved through the busy streets, watching for the two humans.

"How is it not a good idea?" Lore demanded. "This human tears up Benet Aljun'ra' s lounge, and a few hours later there's a hit out on her from Benet's olderling." In the Flexxent language, since one could not be sure if an individual were male or female at any given point in time, siblings were olderlings or youngerlings, denoting their place in the family by age rather than gender.

"And then an arrest warrant. Hits are illegal, Lore."

Lore rolled her eyes. "*Technically* illegal. You and I both know they're not *really* the sort of thing anyone cares about. We have direct instructions not to focus on them anyway."

"That doesn't mean we should start doing them ourselves!"

"It does when it's BSG." She narrowed her eyes at him.

"They're a government office, too. They're just the sort of people you want to have owing you favors."

"No," Rino argued. "No, they're the kind of people you don't want to know you exist."

"You're such a coward. Why are you on the police force?"

Rino decided not to answer that. He walked along in steely silence until they rounded the corner and Lore hissed at him to stop. He ignored her, but she grabbed his arm and dragged him to her side.

When Rino looked up, his eyes got wide.

There were the humans. Facing down two Flexxent cops.

Lore was obviously not the first to have this idea.

"What do we do now?" Rino asked.

"We, uh…" Lore considered.

"Ranger Two, also known as Tabitha." The first officer puffed out his chest. "You are under arrest, by order of—"

"BSG?" one of the humans suggested. The other one was tall and angular, and this one was shorter and had protrusions on the hips and chest.

"Is that the female?" Rino whispered to Lore.

"I think so. I think they're like Torcellans with that. Weird Torcellans with strange coloring. And they're better at building empires." She shrugged.

The two officers who were staring the humans down seemed to be unimpressed with the human's answer.

"By order of the chief of police," the officer finished. "You will come with us now."

"What, you're not going to read me my rights?" Tabitha

crossed her arms and smirked. This officer was all show. He didn't have the guts to attack her.

The Flexxent laughed. "What rights?"

"Well, *this* is new," Ryu murmured. On almost all planets, those being arrested had rights. It was considered the only logical way to do things, given that an innocent person in jail meant a criminal was free on the streets.

"Given that Kenet Aljun'ra runs this place, are you surprised?" Tabitha asked him. She strolled over to the two aliens. "Okay, you're Bloop, and you're Goop. Bloop's done a lot of talking. You want to chime in, Goop?"

The two of them blinked at her.

"Flexxent aren't too bright," Tabitha called over her shoulder.

One of the officers growled, "You are being disrespectful. This will not look good on our report."

"What does it matter if it looks good?" Tabitha was unimpressed. "Seems like the law just decides how things are going to be here. No rules. No rights. And that pisses me off, you know?"

The officer she had nicknamed Goop decided he was done listening to her blather. She was blathering on and on —he had heard that humans did that—and now she was insulting his higher-ups.

To his surprise, the human ducked out of the way of his punch and directed an uppercut at his chest cavity. Goop felt his breath leave him. He stumbled back as his partner tried to tackle her and went flying.

"I bust my ass all day long," Tabitha spoke aloud as she walked around, "risking my very tender ta-tas I will add, and even when a criminal is *obviously* a criminal, I bring them in to stand trial. They face *Justice.* But out here, you all just decide when you think a person should be in jail or get a hit put on them and you take them out like under-handed little bitches that you are. Is the plan for me to get into jail where I won't be able to escape when all the assassins show up?"

"No," replied the first officer, the one she had nick-named Bloop. "The *plan* is for you to die before you get to jail."

"Well, thank you for explaining that. It makes things a lot easier on my end." Tabitha gave him a sweet smile. "Now I don't have to pull my punches."

She ducked and Ryu came up over her back with a leap, slamming an elbow down at Goop's head. The Flexxent staggered back and Bloop grabbed for Ryu, momentarily forgetting Tabitha.

"Oh, no you don't!" Tabitha grabbed his arm and swung off it, pulling the cop around in a big, stumbling circle. "OH MY GOD Wheeeeee!" She let go of him, let him stagger a few more feet, and then directed a kick at his torso.

Bloop went over with a wheeze.

Ryu, meanwhile, had circled to Goop's other side and waited for him to come into range. The Flexxent bent his head, rubbing the place where Ryu's elbow had come down with one hand.

Good enough. Ryu took two steps, turned, and launched himself into a spinning kick that hit the same point on the officer's skull. Bones cracked, and Goop howled. He hadn't gotten his fingers out of the way, and Ryu had broken several of them.

In the alleyway, Lore and Rino were staring at the confrontation with their mouths hanging open.

"Did you know they could fight like that?" Rino asked, not believing his eyes.

"No." Lore shook her head, almost dazed. "I'm glad those other two got here first. I was pissed when we showed up, but I think we would be getting the shit kicked out of us if they weren't."

Rino nodded in wholehearted agreement, taking a couple of steps backward. "Let's go."

"What?" Lore looked at him like he was crazy. "This is our chance!"

"Are you insane?" Rino hissed. "Do you not see what's happening?" He gestured just in time for Bloop to go flying past and land in a heap against a nearby wall. Both Rino and Lore scrambled into the shadows when the male human approached and sank into a crouch, waiting for Bloop to get up. "We have to leave," Rino whispered.

"No way," Lore shot back. "We wait until they're distracted and we take them down!"

"What about your plan of no one knowing what had really happened? Those two will be able to say what they saw!"

"First of all, that one isn't even conscious," Lore pointed out. Goop was swaying on his feet and fell forward just in time for Tabitha to punch him and knock him back slightly before he fell onto her fist again.

As they watched, his legs collapsed, and he went down with a groan.

"Second of all," Lore continued, "maybe we came upon

them getting killed by the humans. We couldn't save them. So sad."

"Are you kidding me? This is turning into one of those plans where we kill everyone who notices we're killing people! Those never end well!"

Lore sniffed. "That's because you lack commitment."

"No, it's because eventually all the bodies trace back to us! I can't believe I'm getting dragged into this again."

"I can't believe I chose to work with you again." She rolled her eyes. "They didn't prove anything last time."

Ryu, who could hear the conversation very clearly, shook his head slightly as he watched Bloop get to his feet. Ryu bowed elegantly to the Flexxent.

"Perhaps you would like to surrender," he suggested. Insults like this were the ones he most enjoyed giving. Even though most people had not been raised in an environment as strict as his had been, they knew enough to be insulted at the suggestion of abandoning their cause.

However, in Ryu's mind, it was more than that. These were police. They had sworn to protect people, but instead, they were here for the hit money. They had no principles left to cling to. Surrender would not strip them of honor.

They didn't *have* any.

"You're going down," Bloop growled. He spat out some blood and pulled his gun. "You see this? Most powerful gun in the city.

"Heads!" Tabitha yelled, and Ryu ducked. She leapt over his head, entirely horizontal, and slammed into Bloop at waist height. He slammed back into the wall and went limp, his eyes rolling back in his head, and she shook her head at Ryu. "I'd use the Special, but I want to save that for someone better than this. Kenet, maybe."

"Uh-huh. And where's Goop?"

Tabitha jerked her thumb over to where the other officer lay, similarly incapacitated. "Let's go find Kenet."

"One second." Ryu pointed to the alley. "There are two more officers there."

Rino and Lore watched in horror as both humans turned to look at them.

And Lore, panicked, raised her gun and shot at them out of instinct.

"Oh, honey," Tabitha said in the dead silence. Both she and Ryu had ducked and then stood back up. Now she gave the two cops a sweet smile. "That was *such* a mistake."

"Ruuuuuun!" Lore screamed. She turned tail and ran, and Rino followed without a second thought.

Behind them, Tabitha was laughing as she chased behind them. "I can't tell if I'm loving this or I hate it!" she called to Ryu as she ran. "On the one hand, this is kind of fun—like shooting fish in a barrel. I could use an easy win or thirty."

"And on the other hand?" At her side, Ryu was running elegantly, not even winded by his exertions—such as they were.

His clothes were another matter, of course—the suit was probably a lost cause, and his hair looked like he'd been riding in a convertible...in the 1980s.

"On the other hand..." Tabitha replied. She caught up

with the police officer who had shot her and dragged the Flexxent over backward by her collar. She looked at Ryu and said loudly and obviously, "You know when you're having a really bad day, and you just want to *kill* the next person who gets on your nerves?"

Ryu grinned as the other officer disloyally tried to make a break for it. Ryu managed to get a handful of the back of his uniform and dragged him back.

"Yeah," he agreed. "Yeah, I definitely do know what that feels like."

"Don't hurt us!" the second officer pleaded. Ryu thought this one looked like a male.

"Oh, I don't know." Ryu tilted his head to the side. "I heard your whole conversation in the alley, and I have to say, I wasn't impressed with your part of it."

"*What*? I was the one who didn't want to get involved!"

"You said you'd done this before, and let's be honest— we both know you were going to cave and try to kill us."

The officer who had shot at Tabitha sensed her opportunity and made a break for it, scrabbling away after trying to sweep Tabitha's ankles.

"You call that a leg-sweep?" Tabitha yelled. "You wouldn't last a minute in Buenos Aires, turdburger!"

"Ew," Ryu murmured delicately as he broke his officer's nose.

Tabitha gave him a look as she ran after the officer, kicked out her feet and when she stopped rolling, Tabitha dragged her back. "Luckily for *you*," she continued speaking to the moaning female, "I don't kill people who are just dumb—and today I don't even have the time to kill people who are trying to fuck me up, so you might get a pass."

Lore managed to get a punch off, and Tabitha rolled her eyes. She slammed her fist down on Lore eight times in close succession, making use of every bit of her enhanced speed and strength.

Lore gave a warbling scream, the sound bouncing as each hit landed, and lay dazed on the ground while Tabitha stifled her laughter with her hand.

"Oh, that was too funny! Did you hear that? Did you *hear* that?"

Ryu was trying to keep a straight face. "I did, Kemosabe. A most impressive noise. Perhaps you will be able to persuade Kenet Aljun'ra to make the same one later."

"You always know how to cheer me up after a hard day, buddy." She gave him a mock punch in the arm. "All right, fuckfaces, tell me what you know about Kenet Aljun'ra. What kind of defenses does he have on his compound?"

"We don't know," Rino whimpered. "He has his own police force. We aren't allowed to go there, even if there's a call or an alarm or anything."

"He's so hoity-toity he doesn't even want the police to come to his place?" Tabitha whistled. "Yeah, I've met guys like that. Likes to dress very sharp, right? Kills people for little things, so everyone stays scared? Throws his money around and thinks it buys loyalty?"

Both police officers nodded hard.

"That's how he is," Lore agreed.

"We've seen him sometimes at government events," Rino added.

"He's mean," Lore stated. "But everyone wants to be a part of BSG, so they all suck up to him."

"And why do they want to be a part of BSG?" Tabitha's tone was too sweet.

Lore noticed that right away and shut up, but Rino missed the cue.

"Because they can do anything they want," he explained. He'd spent his whole life following the rules, terrified of breaking them and getting told off, but for BSG there *were* no rules. You could do whatever the hell you wanted, and no one got in your way.

Too late, he realized that the humans probably weren't going to be very impressed by this. He tried to think of something to say that would save him.

"Interesting," Tabitha mused, still too sweetly. "Is that why you came out here today?"

Rino hung his head. His nose was bleeding like a faucet, and he just wanted to be gone. He mumbled something. Even *he* couldn't tell what the words were.

"I'm sorry, I didn't quite *hear* that."

He was going to die. Why had he gone in today? He could have stayed home in bed, and Lore wouldn't have been able to talk him into going out to take this job. That would have been so much better.

"I said I'm sorry," Rino blurted.

"Hmph. That's a bad fucking excuse. You two don't get it at all. There are steps to Justice. You think there was any Justice in this hit getting taken out on me?"

Rino and Lore looked at each other and burst out laughing.

Tabitha stood up and scratched her head. "What did I

say that was funny?" she asked Ryu.

"You know, I'm not actually sure?"

"It's just the idea of Justice," Rino gasped.

"In Karkat!" Lore finished. The two of them were alternating between holding their bruised faces and shrieking with laughter.

"Especially with BSG!" Rino added.

"On *Karkat*," Lore repeated, and the two of them laughed even harder...until they looked up and saw Tabitha staring at them, tapping her finger on her arm.

"Not. A funny. Joke." She narrowed her eyes. "I grew up in a place where all the cops were corrupt, you know that? Where they only served the rich. Where they thought it was *funny* if someone asked for justice. I was just a scared little kid. I didn't have anything."

Both Flexxent were silent and kept staring at her.

"You know what the problem with those scared little kids is?" Tabitha cocked her head to the side. "Most of the time, they never make it out of the slums. That's true. But the ones who *do* are dangerous as hell."

Her eyes narrowed. "Like *me*."

Her hand shot out, and she grabbed Lore by the collar. The female Flexxent gasped for air as Tabitha slammed her against the side of the nearest building.

"I don't like you," Tabitha snarled. "You're part of the government. You're here to preserve law and order—to help citizens—and you decided that instead, you'd try to get in good with the bastards who are just putting hits out on people. You know why I'm here?"

Lore tried to say something, but she couldn't talk with

Tabitha's hand against her throat. She shook her head, looking panicked.

"I'm here to track down someone who's stealing supplies and getting settlers killed because they don't have the food and the buildings they need. Since I got here, I've run into nothing but roadblocks, which are being thrown up by the people who *should* be helping me."

She stopped and stared into Lore's face. Lore stared back. Spots were dancing in front of her eyes. It was really impressive how scary a tiny human could be.

"So before I burn every single mansion in this city to the ground and hand over everyone's money to the poor, why don't you start trying to convince me that the government has a single fucking shred of decency left?" Tabitha suggested.

"We could do that anyway," Ryu suggested.

"Believe me, I'm strongly considering it."

"You know who doesn't like things like that?"

"Kenet Aljun'ra?"

"No. Your prospective date."

Tabitha gave Ryu a look. "Yeah, but he's hot."

"You know, Bethany Anne doesn't do that kind of stuff. Neither does Barnabas."

"That *you* know of." With a sniff, Tabitha turned back to Lore and waited.

"I know Kenet has a private building in the middle of the compound," Rino suggested finally. "They say it has tunnels coming out."

"That would track," Ryu said. "It was how Benet got out of the club, after all."

"Good point. Anything else?"

"Well, I understand his guards are all pretty complacent." She wiped some blood off of her face. "He's the biggest thing in town, so no one ever messes with him. They know they couldn't take him on, with so many allies. But I don't suppose that matters to you."

Tabitha nodded. "You're right. It doesn't. Now get out of my sight, both of you, and hope I don't decide you need more *Justice*."

They started walking off, and she called after them, "One more thing!"

Both of them stopped, looking like they wanted nothing more than to keep walking.

"I'll be doing spot checks," Tabitha said. "Coming back here to find out from the citizens whether anything has changed."

The two looked at each other before Lore spoke. "But we're just two people—"

Rino spoke up, "The rest of the police force—"

"You'd better hope you can turn it all around," Tabitha warned, unimpressed. She narrowed her eyes at them, and they turned and worked their pace up to a jog.

"I hate to interrupt," Achronyx cut in, "but I believe I've found Grule."

"*Good*," Tabitha exclaimed savagely. "I feel like punching something right now. *Hard*."

Grule had flown the hovercraft to the abandoned building with his hands shaking. That human should *not* have stood up again.

What if the other one was alive too?

There was no way. Still, he wasn't going to be stupid about this. He was going to hide and figure out what the situation was, and then make sure both of them were dead. Then he was going to collect the bounty and probably retire from his life as a hitman, because this job had scared the crap out of him.

Flexxent were big, and they were hard to kill. Frankly, Grule had never considered that any of his marks could kill him. Lots of species thought they were clever or whatever the hell they told themselves, but when push came to shove...

Smart didn't help when someone shot you in the face. Or pounded your chest cavity flat.

Grule had now met a species who didn't stay down

when he hit them, and he wasn't about to stick around and find out just how much they could take.

He was going to wait, and then throw so much at them that they could not possibly survive it.

He took the tunnels under the abandoned building and emerged in another part of town entirely. Karkat was all jumbled so that it was hard to tell good neighborhoods from bad.

There was the gated community, of course, which housed most of the wildly wealthy, but other than that, you could find good and bad streets, and even good and bad *sides* of the street. Sometimes there were mansions on the top floors of buildings that were otherwise run down. Just built right on top and accessible only by hovercraft while the streets below remained the same.

He didn't expect his marks to be able to find him here, even if they came looking. The thought made him shiver, though.

He headed for one of his safe houses. He didn't have to look where he was going. People on the street took one look at his armor and his weapons and got the hell out of his way.

That was how it *should* be. The strongest ruled. The others—*the weak ones*—fell in line.

He was still annoyed when he punched open the door of the building and started climbing the winding ramps that led up into the darkness. His safe house was on the eighth floor and was stocked with more weapons. He'd chosen this one specifically because of the explosives he had stored here.

A lot of people could take a punch, but *no one* could take

a bomb to the face and stay upright. That was his philosophy. Reassured, he trudged up the stairs and pressed his hand against the biolock.

He stepped into the darkness, closed the door behind him, and was confronted by two red pairs of eyes, staring at him from the darkness.

Grule screamed. It was not a particularly impressive scream—of rage, for instance, or any sort of berserker charge. It was a high-pitched scream like a baby Flexxent might emit. There was a moment of pure, absolute *terror*.

From the darkness, he heard laughter.

"Ryu scared you when he got up, didn't he?" Tabitha asked. She found Grule's scream deeply amusing.

And satisfying.

For one thing, she had never heard that pitch come out of even babies before. She had pre-emptively ended the careers of quite a few would-be rapists, and none of them had screamed like that when she grabbed and squeezed.

Out of something the size of a Flexxent, that scream was nothing short of hilarious.

She took a small globe out of her pocket and flicked a switch on the bottom before throwing it up in the air, where it adhered to the ceiling.

"There. Now you can see us."

"We could see *him* just fine," Ryu complained. "I don't see why we're throwing away that advantage."

"It's sportsmanlike."

Ryu looked at her. "He tried to kill you, I think the boat has already sailed on that one."

"You are so negative sometimes."

Grule didn't wait to see how their mock argument

would play out. He pulled out two pistols and shot both of them repeatedly, screaming at the top of his lungs as he did so.

About halfway through the clips, he was bowled over backward.

"See?" Ryu asked as he wrenched one of the guns out of Grule's hands and started beating him over the head with it.

Dazed, Grule could only watch as the gun kept coming down, bouncing off his forehead. There was a burst of pain in his hand, and he screamed again. The woman had stomped on it and taken his other gun.

"All right, for fuck's sake Ryu, stop playing whack-a-mole," Tabitha admonished him.

"I'm just impressed at this point. I've never seen someone take so many hits and still be conscious."

Grule yelled and grabbed Ryu's collar, pulling him close to punch him with his now-free hand. Ryu's head snapped back, and blood came out of his nose in a fountain—for about a moment, until it miraculously clotted on its own.

What sort of animal had blood that clotted that fast? It would be a walking embolism factory.

"Nanites," Ryu mumbled thickly, sounding very pleased at Grule's expression. "You have no idea what you're up against, do you?"

"Ah, ah, ah, no K-word," Tabitha warned.

"I know the rules!"

Grule flipped a switch on his harness, and several mechs came to life around the room.

She looked around, "Ahhh...Monkey balls!" Tabitha swore. She took a running leap and jumped onto one of them, wrestling with its head to wrench it off. She succeeded, but it was able to target its arm gun at Ryu anyway. "Ryu! Dodgeball time!"

"I preferred whack-a-mole!" He dove for cover behind another mech which tried to swivel around to look behind itself and proceeded to get riddled with bullets by the one Tabitha was riding.

Tabitha managed to pull the arms off the mech this time, figuring she might as well sever the piece with the weapon. The mech kept swiveling as though it was dispensing bullets, but the guns were gone.

"Take their arms!" she called.

"On it!" Ryu ripped an arm off the bullet-riddled mech in front of him and threw it at Grule. It hit the Flexxent in the back of the head, and he yelped. "He's trying to escape!"

"You take care of the mechs, and I'll follow him! Oy, *jackass*—come back here!" Tabitha yelled as she wrenched the door open and followed Grule down the hallway. "We have unfinished business! You wanted to kill me, remember?"

He ran down the ramp, picking up speed as he went. He didn't intend to let her catch him.

"The other one said they were the Ranger!"

"He lied! It's allowed when you're talking to a hitman! Even Barnabas does it!" She boosted her speed. "Come back here! I am not done with you!"

Grule burst out onto the street and looked around himself desperately. Where could he go? Neither direction was particularly good or bad.

Tabitha solved the dilemma by tackling him at high speed. People screamed and scattered as she threw him to the ground face-first and picked his torso up to slam it repeatedly into the dirt.

"You!" She grabbed a leg and flung him up and over, slamming him down.

"Are!" she kicked his ribs, hoping the cracking she heard were his ribs, and not his protective armor as he rolled over.

She jumped up, the apogee of her jump a bit over fifteen feet in the air. Coming down, she angled her knees into his back. "A Fucktard!" she hissed when he coughed up blood after his scream of pain.

"I don't like people who try to kill me," she told him at high volume. "You shot me with some gigantic fucking gun, which fucking *hurt.* My fucking tits may never be the same, and if you ruin *those,* hoooo boy, are you going to hear it! My tits are Helen of fucking Troy! Any human man would go to war for them!"

Ryu, emerging onto the street with his arms full of severed mech gun arms, shook his head at this.

"It was just a job!" Grule choked out, "Not personal!"

Tabitha flipped him over, hauled him upright, and punched him seven times in the face. She stepped out of the way as he fell heavily, face-first.

"I don't care if it was just a job," she told his senseless body. She nudged him with her boot. "Wake up, fucker. Pay attention."

Grule groaned.

She kneeled down by his head, speaking conversationally as those in the street watched the puny human. "You don't get to complain if the people you try to kill don't like it," Tabitha informed him. "And by the way? You can go to any of your little hide-outs, and you'll find there aren't any weapons in them anymore. Enjoy your empty rooms, *bastard*."

She spat on him and adjusted her coat before heading back toward Ryu.

"You look ridiculous carrying all those mech arms. And your face is covered in blood."

"You have a gigantic hole in the back of your jacket, a soot-ring on the front of your shirt, and you're covered in dirt."

"Fuck. No time to change before dealing with Kenet?"

"I don't think so." Ryu set off down the street. "This way."

Grumbling, Tabitha put her hair back into a new ponytail and followed him.

Kenet Aljun'ra's complex was located in the heart of Karkat's gated community. Broad avenues lined with flowering plants and trees wound through the district, and giant mansions hid behind high walls with ornamental spikes along the top. Every building dripped opulence. The amount that had been spent on windows, flourishes on the roofs, statuary, and gardens was staggering.

The amount spent on armed guards and automated security measures was even higher.

Instead of making their presence known by patrolling the streets openly, guards observed the district from secure bunkers. Their cameras were embedded in the walls, statues, and trees of the district. That way, everything could be secure while also appearing to be serene and quiet.

With so many cameras on closed circuits, so many booby traps and trip wires, and so many armed guards, the residents likely believed that no one could sneak in.

They were very, *very* mistaken.

"I think I ripped my pants," Tabitha complained as she tumbled sideways over a wall and landed with a thump in the middle of a flowering bush. She craned to check her back. "*Ugh.* Right over my badonkadonk, too." She stood up, brushed herself off, and gave another look at the ripped cloth. "On second thought, I like that. Just a glimpse. Let's *definitely* go past Dev's place on the way back."

Ryu, who was also brushing himself off, paused at this comment but decided not to say anything.

"I am doing this for the good of the Empire," Tabitha informed him as they snuck across the lawn. It had been child's play for Achronyx to disable the security feeds along the various streets, and they were now in Kenet's compound.

"You're going on dates for the good of the Empire?" Ryu knew that her explanation was going to be ridiculous, but damned if he didn't want to hear it anyway. Tabitha had always been able to brighten the worst of the dark days. Even back on Earth when she was flashing her tits, thinking all of them were gay.

"Yes. My bodaciousness will win us allies who can be won in no other way."

"You realize that this *particular* ally—" he started to say.

Don't tell her! Achronyx warned privately. *I want to see her face when she finds out he never has sex with anyone, and definitely not with humans.*

What if she actually pulls it off, though? Ryu asked the EI reasonably.

Achronyx paused in shocked silence.

"What about this particular ally?" Tabitha asked Ryu. She pulled out her climbing gloves as they approached the wall of the main house, and began to climb. "These are good. Much better than taking the chance of ripping a nail."

"You and your nails." Ryu climbed up the old-fashioned way, finding minuscule holds and swinging himself up the wall.

"If you had nails worth protecting you'd feel the same way about them. How can I hope to explain?" Tabitha sniffed. "Achronyx, where do we go from here?"

"It is impossible to get to Kenet's office from the roof. You will have to go through the hallway, which is patrolled by soldiers, and fight your way there."

"It's *impossible?* Nothing is impossible. You've seen me—"

"It is impossible to do so without attracting attention that will compromise the mission. So many reinforcements will arrive from various guard stations both in the compound and the district that it is highly unlikely you will be able to complete your mission before needing to escape."

"Oh. Why didn't you say so the first time?" Tabitha headed for a skylight. "All right, boys, prepare for one badass *chica.*" She gave Ryu a look. "Maybe my butt will distract them."

"I don't think— *Fine*. Yes. Maybe it will." Ryu decided that agreement was the better part of valor in this case.

"Achronyx, you've turned off all of the alarms, right?"

"Yes, Ranger Tabitha. They will be unable to call for backup."

"Good. GERONIMOOOOOO!" Tabitha took a running leap and punched her way down through the skylight in a hail of falling glass, landing in a hallway with four shocked-looking guards.

"However, it is highly likely that Kenet Aljun'ra heard that."

"Why didn't you warn me?"

"I should have thought it was obvious that I am not able to remotely disable ears on organic beings."

"*Listen*, smarty-pants." Tabitha ducked as the first guard brought his gun up. His mouth was still hanging open, but he was trained to shoot intruders, and she was *definitely* an intruder.

He didn't get a chance to do any real damage. She took off down the corridor, staying low and zig-zagging to keep out of his line of fire, and arrived in time to knock him out with a spinning kick to the head.

She grabbed the gun and used it to bludgeon the second guard while Ryu dispatched the other two. Ryu's strikes were precise and elegant as he hit them in the throat and struck pressure points that made the Flexxent guards double over in pain.

Ryu and Tabitha took thin coils of reinforced rope out of their pockets and restrained all four guards. The guards thrashed, but they were not able to reach the knots. Tabitha placed tiny lozenges on each of their tongues. The lozenges swelled to become gags that would not interfere with breathing, but that would have a sound-dampening effect.

The guards stared at her in panic as she and Ryu went to the door of Kenet's study. A few were jerking and struggling in particular ways that were likely supposed to press hidden buttons and summon help.

Tabitha didn't bother to tell them that it wouldn't do any good. They would figure it out sooner or later on their own.

"Here's the plan," she told Ryu, smirking slightly. "We go in there and blow his head right off."

Ryu frowned at her. "Are you making a joke?"

Her face scrunched up. "No, I'm totally serious. He's a reprehensible *jackass*."

"We have a process, Kemosabe," Ryu said uncertainly.

"You and your *process*." Tabitha wiggled her fingers and rolled her eyes before pounding on the door with all her might. "Kenet Fuckface'ra! Open up!"

Ryu groaned and dropped his head into one hand.

The door didn't open, and Tabitha sighed as she went back to pick up one of the guards. She slammed him against the door feet-first until the door began to give way, finally breaking and sending the guard shooting out of her hands to sprawl on the ornate carpet in Kenet's office.

She pointed into the office. "You see how merciful I'm being?" Tabitha demanded as she kicked down the last of the door and marched inside. "I let him be a battering ram *feet*-first."

"Truly, your mercy will be sung of by the bards," Ryu commented.

"That's enough sass from you, Ryu-toshi. And *you*," Tabitha added to Kenet, who was trying to make a break for his panic room. She pulled out her Jean Dukes Special and let the hammer click back. "Make one. More. Move, and I will make a Jackson Pollock of your blood on that wall."

Kenet froze. He didn't know what a Jackson Pollock was, but he had the distinct sense that he didn't want to try this woman's patience. She had gotten into his compound, and she should *not* have been able to do that.

Then she had broken down his study doors…using one of his guards. She had done everything so far without even using a gun, so he wasn't going to mess around when she was pointing one at him.

Yet.

"What do you want?" he asked her. He straightened up and adjusted his cuffs imperiously. Mayors, governors, elected officials, bah! Kenet Aljun'ra *ran* Karkat, and everyone knew it.

He was not about to be intimidated by some tiny human in torn pants.

"I want to know why you put a hit out on me," Tabitha replied, jabbing the gun at him. "Do you always use government black ops to take out people who mess up your little brother's bar?"

"No." Kenet returned to his desk and made a show of sitting down. "Please, take a seat. Let us have this discussion civilly."

"Nuh-uh. Civility went out the window when you put a hit out on me." Tabitha gave a sarcastic smile and kept the gun pointed at him. "Hands where I can see 'em, Gigantor."

Kenet made a show of spreading his hands. He stared Tabitha down.

"All right," Tabitha continued. "Let's get one thing clear. In the past few days, I have been shot in the back more than once and shot in the *front* by people you paid to kill me. I have been thrown off roofs. I have been chased by cops who literally fell down laughing at the idea of Justice in Karkat." She gestured to Ryu, who was also bloodied and covered in dirt and grime. "You can see from our clothes what we've been through in the past few hours alone. So why don't you give me an explanation of what you think you were up to, or I swear to God I'll make sure you experience every bit of it."

"Kemosabe, I don't think he would survive that," Ryu murmured. "We should not pretend that we do not follow the rules of Justice."

Tabitha shot him a look before staring back at Kenet. "Well? Get talking!"

"You are a wanted woman, Ranger Two." Kenet raised an eyebrow. "Surely you know that. When a human came into Benet's lounge and caused considerable damage, I was interested. Humans have long been known to be inconvenient. They cause trouble. I contacted some friends to see if they had any information on this particular human, and they did. They also had requests, namely, to make sure you couldn't keep causing trouble. I did my best to oblige them." For the first time, his pleasant mask slipped. "Unfortunately, you appear to be difficult to kill."

"Oh, you have no idea, cupcake," Tabitha replied.

Without warning, an electrified net dropped from the ceiling and Kenet ran for the exit.

"Achronyx! Sonofa—"

"Neutralizing." Achronyx cut power to the relevant circuit.

Tabitha threw the net off her and ran to intercept Kenet. He had the door open when she grabbed him and shoved him hard, using his existing momentum to propel him headfirst into a bookshelf. Alien dictionaries rained down on his cranium as she flung him over one shoulder onto the ground and directed a punch at the area where his sternum should be.

"I am so tired of people thinking they can get a leg up on me with sneaky tricks!" she complained.

Kenet grabbed her hands.

"And I am so tired of these motherfucking Flexxent being so motherfucking hard to knock out!" she added. She hauled at her hands before he could crush them, as he obviously intended to. One finger *had* snapped, and she shook her hand out while it healed, directing a kick at his face to keep him down in the meantime. "Ryu, please take care of this underhanded bastard while my finger heals."

"With pleasure, Kemosabe." Ryu hauled Kenet up and slammed him face-first over the desk, holding his arms in a lock. "Try anything else," he advised pleasantly, "and you will be taken back to Empire space, where you will face the Empress' justice. I assure you that you do not want that." Ryu continued speaking as Tabitha was sucking on her finger. "My Empress has little compassion. She would probably listen to about the first paragraph of your crimes and then casually throw you out into space to walk home. I understand breathing is a tad difficult."

Tabitha, still shaking her hand and cursing, looked at all the plush carpets and came to a conclusion.

"Achronyx, can you get into his computer systems?"

"I am insulted by that question. I am already in."

"Oh, really?" Tabitha gave a mischievous grin and switched to speaking silently. *All right, pull everything he has. And also...*

She gave instructions and listened as Achronyx carried them out. Ryu, who was also listening, laughed at some of them.

Finally, Tabitha plugged in a security stick and entered a few commands of her own. She gestured for Ryu to let Kenet up and held the stick out to him.

"I've instructed my EI to take most of what you have. It will be distributed appropriately to the people you have ripped off and exploited, starting with the people you had build this district. Yeah, that's right, we can see that you didn't pay them."

Kenet took the stick and plugged it into his computer. When he saw the number of credits, his jaw dropped. "That is barely enough to keep me for a month!"

"That's with how you live now, asswipe. You have enough in there to live a year like a normal person, which is more than enough time to come up with a new way to make a living. I'm being extremely generous. Who the hell needs heated toilets with custom settings that activate from a bioscan? Who *needs* a dining room that has weather systems and a forcefield to keep any rain from getting in the food?"

"I can't live on this!" Kenet was panicking, his eyes large. "I won't be able to maintain my security force!"

"Too bad, so sad. You should work on making people like you better." Tabitha tilted her head at him with a shrug.

"You don't understand my position! I have to maintain all this to be respected!"

Ryu's patience snapped, he pulled his own Jean Dukes and placed the tip against his skull, surprising Tabitha. "You have Option One, which is essentially a free ride for a year. Option Two is, I blow your brains out."

Kenet swallowed. "I will take Option One."

"I knew you would see reason," Tabitha purred. "We have your info. If you go back after the money? Ryu will be back without me to stop him."

She swept out of the room and jumped on two large statues to get back to the skylight. She sashayed along the roof, trying to cut open the other side of her pants with a piece of broken glass.

When Ryu caught up with her, she smirked at him.

"Why didn't you threaten to bring him in and blow his brains out?" Ryu demanded. "Once we got in there, you started being too nice."

"Achronyx and I had a bet going on whether your much-vaunted patience had a limit." Tabitha's smirk grew wider. "I won!"

"You're *kidding* me." Ryu followed her to the main part of the city, where they flagged a taxi. "To the docks, please," he told the driver. Achronyx had told them that he was bringing the ship back to the original port now that the hit had been rescinded.

Ryu looked at himself. "This is filthy!"

"There will be a dirty tax for all the blood and dirt you

are getting on the seats," the taxi driver told them from behind a bulletproof screen.

"What a crook!" Tabitha exclaimed. "Let's get out of this city. I am so done with this place."

"You're forgetting something," Ryu informed her.

"What?"

"Etoy Walce." He didn't feel like reminding her about Dev Zancred right about now.

"Noooo." Tabitha slumped forward in her seat. "He better be easy to find, because I am not going to stay much longer. I want to find out just who asked Kenet to put a hit on me. And find them."

"You will be unsurprised to learn that it was a Skaine pirate."

"Right. We get Etoy, throw him in the brig, and then go *find* that Skaine bastard." Tabitha got out of the taxi as it pulled to a stop. "*Gott Verdammt*, my pants stuck to the seat. I don't want to know what was on it! Achronyx, pay the extortionate dirty tax and remind me never to take a taxi again."

CHAPTER 16 TABITHA

An hour later, showered and dressed in yet another set of clean clothes, Tabitha and Ryu sat in her rooms talking with Hirotoshi on a video call. Their experiences on Karkat so far had not been promising, and Tabitha had not yet decided what she wanted to do about Etoy Walce.

"I don't know." She sighed at the screen. "I think the government here is behind most of the people who are doing shady things. They are probably aware of what Walce is doing, and they are giving him a free pass because he helps them cut costs on maintaining the infrastructure."

"That is probably how Walce has stayed in business so long." Hirotoshi nodded. "He works *for* the governments. They pay him to steal food and materials. I thought perhaps he was selling those things, but I think he is just taking a large cut of the profits from each government when he gives them the goods."

Ryu nodded. "The government here would definitely support something like that," he agreed. "They don't care to spend money on making people's quality of life higher. They just want to do enough to stave off riots."

"Unfortunately, it seems clear that he has a lot of connections," Hirotoshi said. He looked at the two of them. "What are you two going to do?"

"Excuse me," Achronyx cut in verbally. "I am also a member of this team."

Hirotoshi nodded. "I am sorry, Achronyx. What are you *three* going to do?"

"Don't encourage him," Tabitha warned. "He likes to make snide remarks and insult Ryu and me. And he doesn't understand the importance of sex in politics."

Hirotoshi blinked and considered this. "I do not want to know what that means," he decided finally.

"Oh! See, so I found this *gorgeous* guy when we were going through the—"

"Are there any resources you require, Kemosabe?" Hirotoshi asked, speaking over Tabitha. He paused. "I apologize, I believe our connection was shaky for a moment. I did not mean to interrupt you. I do want to make sure you can pull off the mission with what you have there, however. We could meet you on the planet if you needed us to do so, or you could rendezvous with us here."

Ryu noted how Hirotoshi had redirected the conversation and smirked. So *this* was how Hirotoshi kept Tabitha on track during missions. Ryu knew that Hirotoshi also listened to many hours of similar discussions in good humor when they were off-mission.

None of the Tontos could ever have imagined serving someone like Tabitha. First, because she was a woman, and second, because of her entire attitude toward life.

However, Tabitha's sense of Justice had demonstrated the value of finding allies beyond the expected. They had learned to broaden their horizons and accept leaders by their qualities, not by the arbitrary markers of respect used in the old world.

Also, her sense of humor was surprisingly infectious.

Tabitha had been thinking about Hirotoshi's words and was chewing her lip meditatively. "I don't think we should wait for backup," she announced finally. "I think this mission is something Ryu-toshi and I can accomplish on our own if we plan things correctly. Yes, and the grumpy EI as well," she added before Achronyx could cut in again.

"Ryu-toshi?" Hirotoshi asked, confused.

"I think he might be you in disguise," Tabitha explained. "Or you've possessed him, so you could keep an eye on me or something. But the old Ryu is in there. I'm cracking him out piece by piece. I got him to threaten to blow that guy's brains out, for instance. That's *real* progress."

Hirotoshi was speechless.

"Anyway," Tabitha continued, smiling at his dumbstruck expression, "Achronyx thinks Walce is still on the planet."

"Correct," Achronyx agreed. "He seems to believe that because he has evaded Ranger Tabitha so far, he can continue to do so. In many ways, Karkat provides more of an obstacle to her doing so than there would be on another planet, or in space."

Hirotoshi frowned. "Shouldn't we wait to take him on in another location, then?"

"No," Tabitha argued, "because if we wait, he might steal more things or run away. We can get to him, we just have to be mindful of how this city works. We have had many misunderstandings, but I think we can plan around those and capture him before he has the chance to do any more damage."

"This guy is doing shit across multiple worlds," Ryu added. "Empire worlds included. He has to go down."

"I don't disagree," Hirotoshi said doubtfully. "I simply want you two to be prepared. I think perhaps I should—"

"You're already here." Tabitha jerked her head at Ryu. "So there's no problem."

Ryu and Hirotoshi both glared at her.

"We're perfectly capable of coming up with a plan on our own," Tabitha offered serenely. "We'll be out of here in two days tops, with Walce in the brig. And as soon as I drop him off for a dose of actual justice, we can go out and catch this Skaine bastard who's getting people to put hits out on me!"

"I meant to ask about that," Hirotoshi murmured. "You said you were targeted by Karkat's black ops on a request of Skaines?"

"It's complicated, but yes. This is the sort of thing that *won't* happen once I put my plan of date warfare into action."

Hirotoshi nodded gracefully. "I see. I look forward to seeing you again soon, Kemosabe. Ryu, Achronyx. If there is nothing more I can do, I will leave you to your planning."

He terminated the call, and Tabitha grinned at Ryu.

Tabitha raised her eyebrows. "He shouldn't be so dismissive of my *physical* strategy. These curves can cause universal peace if deployed correctly."

"I thought the lesson from human history was that the

result of any horizontal *physical* strategy was invariably chaos."

Tabitha didn't miss a beat with her response. "We ended the call, Hirotoshi. Why are you still here?"

Ryu groaned. "I am *Ryu*."

"So you say, but do you have any evidence of that? I thought not." She turned in her seat. "Now, Achronyx, what can you tell us about Etoy Walce?"

"I hesitate to tell you," Achronyx replied. "I fear you will use my information in worrisome ways."

"Now you *have* to tell me. I'm very interested!"

Ryu looked up apprehensively as Achronyx explained, "Etoy Walce will be attending a ball. It is the first event of Karkat's social season. I believe the two of you can obtain invitations and apprehend him there."

"A ball?" Tabitha exclaimed. "We can dress up and dance? Will Dev be there?"

"I am unsure if Mr. Zancred will attend."

"Get him an invite, too! Say it's compliments of..." Tabitha considered. "BB."

"BB?" Ryu asked her.

"Bodacious Babe." Tabitha tossed her hair. "Achronyx, get us details on that ball so we can make a plan. I'm going to get our guy, and then I'm going to have the best date ever."

"The ball is tonight," Tabitha stated. She crossed her arms and stared at the holoimages of the ballroom. "Unfortunately, no one is going to get there until about midnight, so we have to wait to snag our guy."

"Wouldn't it make sense to snag him on the way to the party?" Ryu asked.

"Nuh-uh. With so many dignitaries attending, no one's going to want to shoot if it's clear we don't intend to hurt anyone else. They'll let him go with us." Tabitha grinned. "That's if they even notice he's gone. He's not Dev. He's not going to have women falling all over him."

"How do you know? Etoy Walce might be a prime specimen of male beauty by the standards of the other females at the ball."

Tabitha shuddered. "He looks like a rat. Anyway, I figured we'd go in, do some dancing, wait for him to show up—it might be a while, or we might just be able to grab him and go—and then we take the roof out of there."

"Hold on. I believe I feel a responsibility to remind you that roofs have *not* been our friend on this mission." Ryu snorted. "Last time, you forgot to use your harness and wound up with a broken leg, *and* got disoriented, so we went to the wrong building."

"No, *last* time I got us into Kenet's compound, and we went out the same way without me falling even once."

"Hmm." Ryu had to admit she was correct on that point. "The time before last, though—"

"I got knocked *off* the roof and cleverly used my situational awareness to find a gargoyle to hold onto while I healed."

"And what did you learn from getting knocked off the roof?"

"To plan the assault with you." Tabitha rolled her eyes,

but Ryu knew she was actually chastened. "You made good points. We would probably have avoided a lot of trouble if I had let you sneak up on him first. I don't know how many times on this mission I would have benefited from listening to you."

"Three come to mind immediately," Achronyx chimed in. "If we are counting me as a member of the team. We do not seem to be doing that all the time."

"It's hard to remember you when you aren't visible," Tabitha explained, waving her hand in a circle. "Don't get all...*you know*...about it." She finished lamely.

"I do not know."

Tabitha covered her mouth. "Achronyx, it's not important right now. Planning the mission is important. Mostly because we've just gotten to the best part." She clapped her hands. "What we get to wear! Achronyx, what *do* we get to wear?"

"I have done research and reviewed holos from last year's ball compared to current fashion trends, and I am pleased to report that we have suitable clothing already aboard the ship, except for some small accents I have taken the liberty of ordering. Karkat follows Torcellan fashion trends since many of the nobles are Torcellan. Your outfits are waiting for you in your respective rooms."

"Do we have any further details to—" Ryu began, but Tabitha was already gone.

"I'm going to get dressed up!" she yelled as she ran toward her rooms.

Ryu sighed and spoke aloud. "I hope there was nothing more we needed to plan."

"I hope so as well," Achronyx replied. "Next time, I will be careful to ascertain that before mentioning clothes."

Ryu strolled out of his rooms an hour later, dressed in a suit of rich blue with gold filigree epaulets on the shoulders. Similar accents adorned the lapels of the suit, the pocket, and his cuffs.

"This is quite the outfit," he commented to Achronyx. "However, I have doubts about my hair."

In Torcellan fashion, his hair had been dressed very elaborately, after having been dyed a silvery blond. In Ryu's opinion, even though his skin had been painted a cooler tone to match, none of it went very well with his features.

"I thought it was important that your appearance not arouse suspicion," Achronyx replied. "I will make a show of blasting off a few hours before the party so that our target will not think we are still here. No one who looks closely at you will confuse you for a Torcellan, but Etoy Walce will not know to run as soon as you come into the room."

"I don't understand how he would pick us out of the crowd if it's filled with many different types of aliens," Tabitha chimed in. She was still in her rooms getting ready, but she was paying attention to the discussion. "And I'm with Ryu, Achronyx—I have a beef with what you picked out for me."

"I assure you, Ranger Tabitha, all of this was done with much care."

"I've seen how you do things. You like to be sneaky! What are people going to think when they look at us?"

Ryu had to admit this was a good question.

Achronyx sounded a bit too smug when he replied, "They will think you are a visiting Torcellan nobleman and his wife."

"What?" Ryu looked up.

"Hey!" Tabitha yelled at the same time. "Listen, Achronyx, Dev might be there, and I am *not* going to sabotage my chances of getting a date with him!"

"I believe extramarital affairs are common within the Torcellan nobility. Furthermore, to answer your questions about looks, even though Karkat is technically a Flexxent city, the Torcellans make up the bulk of the nobility and control almost all of the government. Kenet Aljun'ra was an anomaly in that regard. There will be only one or two token non-Torcellans at the ball tonight. Unless you disguise yourselves, you have no *hope* of blending in."

Ryu grimaced, but he had to accept that Achronyx's reasoning was sound. He sat in the copilot's chair on the bridge as he waited for Tabitha. "Are there any customs we should follow as a married couple?"

"Yes," Achronyx told them. "In Torcellan culture, the woman is the primary. The man is considered an accessory."

Ryu looked up sharply, and Tabitha chuckled, her eyes dancing with mischief.

She jerked a thumb in his direction. "He's an accessory? Ryu, did you hear that? You're an accessory! I hope you're in fashion this year. I'd hate to show up with *last* year's trends."

"I hope you understand what you have subjected me to," Ryu murmured to Achronyx.

"I do. Unfortunately, it was unavoidable."

"You had better be right about that."

Tabitha was still shaking her head. "So, how should Ryu behave as an *accessory*?"

"Perhaps 'ornament' would be a better word," Achronyx suggested.

"Achronyx, you are not making this better," Ryu told him.

"Ah. My regrets. You will likely not enjoy the rest of this explanation, either. As the secondary partner, the male Torcellan is expected to make the female happy in every way."

"Happy wife, happy life!" Tabitha called. "Even Torcellans know that, Ryu."

Ryu was sitting in his chair with an expression of resignation.

"And remember, we're Rangers. We have to give our efforts our *all*." Tabitha swept onto the bridge. Her hair and skin had also been changed to Torcellan coloring. "You have to make me happy, Ryu," she repeated as she twirled around. "You have to do everything to make sure Etoy Walce doesn't know we aren't really Torcellan until we nab him. Oh, this is going to be so fun. You have to make *me*—"

She broke off, staring at Ryu. She had finally caught sight of him.

"Hey!" Her voice was furious. "That is *not* fair!"

Ryu finally looked up—and choked on his laughter.

Tabitha's dress was beige. Just beige. No ornamentation. It was not particularly well fitted, either.

"As the primary," Achronyx explained, sounding very

smug, "the female is expected to manage business concerns. The *male* is expected to be ornamental."

"You know, Achronyx," Ryu mused, "I think I might just enjoy this ball after all." He stood up with a flourish and bowed to Tabitha. "Shall we go? I believe both of us look... appropriate to our roles."

"Listen." Tabitha glared at him and all of the pretty aspects of his clothes. "You are not making me very happy right now, *secondary partner.*"

Ryu snorted.

"I still say this is bullshit," Tabitha muttered a little while later as they made their way into the packed ballroom arm in arm. "My dress is so bland that mud looks good in comparison."

"You're not wrong," Ryu agreed. "At least mud has some color to it. Did they even put dye on that dress?"

"Keep your chin up and smile, *honey.*" Tabitha clenched his hand as hard as she could.

"Ow! I'm sorry...*sweetie.*" Ryu tried not to wince as Tabitha crushed his hand. "Cupcake? Snookums? Light of my life?"

Tabitha looked to her right. "Ornamentation doesn't talk, Ryu."

B*e careful to keep your expression calm, Ranger Tabitha,* Achronyx cautioned. *Torcellan women, especially here, are expected to stay calm, cool, and collected.*

"If we're the primary partners, why don't we get to do any of the fun stuff?" Tabitha complained.

Achronyx replied. "I believe the 'fun stuff,' as you call it, is reserved for the males."

Ryu gave a sleek, self-satisfied smile.

"I didn't even know there were this many Torcellans on the planet. Why didn't we see more than one or two in the city?" Tabitha asked.

As the ruling class, they rarely emerge from the gated district.

"Someone's gunning for a revolution," Tabitha muttered.

"Yeah, well, talk it out with your boy toy," Ryu suggested. "He helped install the current regime."

"I *should* talk to him about it!" Tabitha agreed excitedly.

"I regret bringing it up."

"No, it was a good idea. Especially coming from the secondary partner." She patted his arm. "Take a few minutes to recover from the exertion."

Ryu glowered.

"Excuse me, Lady Yerev?" A butler bowed in front of Tabitha. "The trade delegation to Karkat 5c has asked to speak with you."

"Of course," Tabitha responded. She swept along, bringing Ryu with her until the butler stopped her with wide eyes.

"My lady, it would be entirely inappropriate for Lord Yerev to hear such things."

Male Torcellans would not be involved in a business discussion, Achronyx chimed in.

"I beg your pardon, of course. I'm known to be quite eccentric." Tabitha smiled brilliantly.

That is one way of describing it, Ryu said internally.

Shut up, Ryu. "Go and dance, sweetie." Tabitha sent him

off with a pat on the arm. *Achronyx? Want to explain what's going on?*

I have told the nobility that you are Weda Yerev, a trade dignitary from Karkat 5c, Achronyx explained as Tabitha made her way across the room.

This person actually exists? Tabitha fought the urge to send an annoyed glance at Achronyx. She wasn't sure exactly where Achronyx was, so she would have to settle for "up." *What if someone knows her and exposes me? Did you think of that?*

I chose someone who is a known eccentric, as you told the butler. I assumed from that statement that you had read the brief I prepared.

Gott Verdammt briefs! "Well, I didn't."

Achronyx gave a mechanical sigh. *I see. That must have been a lucky guess. Yerev, whose name interested me because it is an old Torcellan word for night, and thus reminded me of Nacht, never emerges from her estates outside the city. She is always sent invitations but always declines them. I did not secure you an invitation—I took hers.*

You realize I now have to carry on a conversation about trade between the various parts of Karkat. What is Karkat 5c?

The third moon on the fifth planet. The system is also known as Karkat.

In addition to the city? This is ridiculous.

I could not agree more. Now, remember to act very proper and without much emotion.

It's not enough that Ryu is Hirotoshi now, I have to be Hirotoshi as well?

It might be good for you.

Eat shit and have a CPU heat meltdown. Tabitha smiled at the EI's confused silence and glided up to the group of dignitaries, all of whom bowed.

Put your left hand on your left shoulder and bow your head, Achronyx instructed.

Are we going to do this for the whole discussion?

Yes, you'll have to pay attention for once.

"Lady Yerev," said a Torcellan female. Tabitha was pleased to see that she was wearing an equally bland dress. If anything, it was less well fitted. It resembled a potato sack, but with no logo to give it any sort of pattern.

Call her "counselor."

"Counselor," Tabitha replied. She tried to use the tone she imagined Hirotoshi would use. *I sound like a prat.*

You sound like a well-bred noble lady.

With a stick up my ass.

"We wanted to discuss the regrettable trade situation on 5c," another lady said. She had—scandalously, Tabitha imagined—worn a black bracelet to go along with her dress.

The mines on 5c have run out of ore. Tell them that you have survey teams coming close to another rich vein.

"I understand your concerns," Tabitha improvised, "but I'm pleased to report that I have survey teams presently coming close to another rich vein."

The ladies murmured appreciatively.

"We didn't realize that," one of them exclaimed. "Lady Yerev, why didn't you say so as soon as the news broke?"

"I knew the trade delegation would not be swayed by mere rumors," Tabitha explained airily. "The only sensible thing to do was find new locations for ore, of course. You would assume that was what I was doing. Why worry about such a thing?"

The ladies looked at one another, but none of them wanted to admit that they had been anxious instead of assuming that things would proceed according to a sensible plan.

"Of course, Lady Yerev," the first one agreed finally.

Tabitha smiled beatifically, as she had often seen Hirotoshi do.

They're eating it up.

Yes, good job. Achronyx sounded long-suffering. *Now compliment them on the punch and say you're so glad other people have discovered the jori fruit at long last.*

You had better not be paying a practical joke on me. Tabitha looked at the refreshments table. "May I say, I am *so* glad other people have discovered the jori fruit at last. I thought I was the only one! But the punch is absolutely divine."

The ladies stared at her with their mouths hanging open.

Excuse yourself to look after Ryu. No normal noblewoman would do that, but you have an eccentric reputation to uphold.

"If you'll excuse me now," Tabitha said, giving the same gesture of respect she had before, "I'm going to go watch my husband dance."

Torcellan women do not watch the men dance while they're doing business, Achronyx explained to her as she walked away. *They don't usually dance at all during balls. And regarding the juice, the jori fruit was just found on an uninhab-*

ited planet three months ago. *You were hinting at having known the location of the planet for years and drinking the juice without even bothering to sell it.*

I like that!

Tabitha pushed her way through the crowd and eventually found the knot of dancers. There, she could only shake her head.

Ryu was dancing once again.

Ryu flashed her a smile. Achronyx had instructed him to behave like a pampered nobleman indulged by Tabitha. When a group of other noblemen had begun dancing, Achronyx had suggested joining in—and getting everyone's attention by being a fantastic dancer and adding flourishes to the otherwise stately measures.

So Ryu was now doing a solo in the middle of what was supposed to be a circle dance.

With his years of training in combat he had picked out the footwork effortlessly, and now he was riffing on the patterns he'd seen in the nightclub as well as the circle dance itself.

People seemed to like it. They were swaying in time to the music, and Ryu gave a last twirl and finished with an extravagant bow.

You know, he said privately to Tabitha and Achronyx, *I could get used to this.*

Just let me be there to see Bethany Anne's face when you tell her you're quitting the team to be a Torcellan dancer, Tabitha said wickedly. *Ryu, let's be extra-scandalous and leave the main room. I want to do a scan of the area and find our guy.*

"Well, that was a disaster," Tabitha grumbled in English as they swept across the floor. Everyone was watching them, and she fought the urge to swish her hips. "Torcellan females never get to do anything fun."

"Don't worry, I'm doing all the badonkadonk-swaying for both of us," Ryu replied.

Tabitha pressed her lips together and tried not to howl with laughter. "I am *trying* to channel Hirotoshi, and you say shit like that."

"He has to be that way when *you* say things like that." Ryu countered.

"Good point," Tabitha conceded. "I only got away with that meeting because those ladies knew I was eccentric."

She did very well, Achronyx chimed in.

Tabitha's eyes widened. *Was that praise, Achronyx? With a complete lack of snark?*

I believe in giving credit where credit is due. You "channeled Hirotoshi," as you put it, and were very convincing.

"Will wonders never cease!" Ryu exclaimed, wide-eyed. "Meanwhile, I channeled you," he told her.

"And got to do all the fun stuff. I'm going to be bitter about that for ages. We get to go to a ball, *you* get this amazing suit, and I have to dress in what looks like a rice bag."

Ryu chose to look her up and down. "A washed-out rice bag."

Tabitha resisted the urge to glare at him. They were circling the outside of the room, and she still had to look serene and calm. Eccentricity would only go so far.

Etoy Walce is close to the fountains on the other side of the room, Achronyx reported. *I've found him on the security cameras. He is drinking punch and hoping that the minister of commerce will come to talk to him.*

Why doesn't he go talk to him?

Her. Because it is a ball, and he is an unaccompanied male. He cannot initiate the discussion.

But I could?

Yes. I would advise getting him to run if you can, however. Then you cannot be charged with abduction.

Tabitha nodded and guided Ryu around the room.

He is wearing the green suit, Achronyx said.

"Oh, good," Tabitha muttered as she dodged a waiter. "We're hunting a leprechaun."

Ryu laughed. "Let's hope he doesn't have the luck o' the Irish."

"Let's hope he has a pot of gold! Or some Lucky Charms. Man, I could *really* go for some Lucky Charms." She looked at Ryu, sadness on her lips for a moment before it disappeared. "You miss things about Earth, you know?"

"All right, if we want to get him to leave before we do, why don't we flank him?" Tabitha suggested.

"Oh, you mean just be very obvious about it?" Ryu asked.

"Exactly. He will think he's seen us first. We'll be set up well enough that he'll *have* to run, and he'll go right out that door over there."

"Good call."

Achronyx? Anything you want to weigh in with?

No, for once I think this is a solid plan.

You're beginning to creep me out, Tabitha informed him. She nodded to her left. "You go that way, I'll go to the right. When I reach that potted palm, you start heading for him and kind of push people out the way so he can see the disturbance in the crowd."

Ryu nodded, and they split up to approach Etoy Walce. Their target was a small Torcellan male with a very pointy face. He was dressed more finely than most of the noble males there. When Tabitha asked why that was, Achronyx explained that because Etoy did not have a mate, he would have to attract one—hence the display.

He was allowed to wear multiple colors in the same garment. Ryu was of the opinion that it looked ridiculous.

That's just because you think he's outdoing you, Tabitha told him. *I'm in position. Let's go.*

They began moving through the crowd in unison. On the wall behind the refreshments table, large windows showed the skyline of Karkat. From the gated district the city looked remote, but it glittered nicely with lights.

They had not gotten very far when Walce looked up and noticed the disturbance. He glanced at Ryu and then at Tabitha, and his eyes narrowed as he assessed them. Then he turned and ran. But he did not run for the doorway at the end of the room, as they had guessed he would.

He shattered a window near him and jumped out instead.

"Holy shitballs!" Tabitha took off, shoving her way through the crowd. The orchestra had stopped playing, and now that the window was broken, the sounds of the city were filtering in.

"Remember your harness this time!" Ryu yelled as they both made for the window.

Achronyx! Which way did he go?

He jumped to the roof of the next building over, straight ahead, and is now running along the roof.

"I don't need a harness for that! Let's gooooooo!" Tabitha jumped, hit the roof, and tumbled less elegantly than she had expected to. "Fuck, I forgot I was wearing heels! And a skirt!" She pulled the skirt up as she ran.

"Take the time to switch to shoes!" Ryu called to her. He tossed her a pair of what were essentially boot soles that would adhere to the bottoms of her feet. "I brought these for you in case we needed to run!"

"There's one cool-looking thing about my outfit, and I'm not going to spoil it!" Tabitha had found her stride and was enjoying the moonlit chase. She pulled one of her guns out of her thigh holster and pointed at Walce. "Keep him going this direction. We're herding him to the ship."

The two of them began to use their shots not to hit Walce, but to keep him going in a roughly straight line across the rooftops. From here, it was almost a straight line to the loading docks.

Walce seemed to know what they were doing, however, and he was a very quick runner. He made a sudden turn and leapt up to grab the gargoyles that adorned the side of a taller building next to the one he was on. He climbed up through the gargoyles, knowing that they would not shoot at him when he was climbing past windows.

"Damn!" Tabitha followed him and began to climb. "I should have brought my climbing gloves."

"You have no pockets," Ryu objected.

"This dress is a shapeless sack. I could have gotten away with it." She was panting as she climbed. *Achronyx, is he on the roof?*

Not yet.

Just then, Walce began to shoot down at them. Tabitha cursed and slipped as the gargoyle she was holding exploded into stone chips. Several hit her in the chest, leaving bleeding wounds that began to shrink at once as she grabbed for another hold and began climbing again.

"I do *not* like this guy."

Ryu glanced a look over. "On the plus side, your dress looks more interesting with holes and blood."

"That's true." Tabitha looked up in time to see Walce disappear over the top of the roof. *Achronyx, where do we go from here?*

He is going directly across the roof to try to lose you.

"Like hell!" Tabitha redoubled her efforts and hauled herself onto the roof. She tore off her heels and put on a burst of vampiric speed.

Walce looked back and saw her as she came over the

edge of the roof. He had just landed on the roof one building ahead, and his eyes went wide when he saw her. He pulled his gun back out and began to shoot as she came toward his roof.

Worse, he was a good shot.

Tabitha, seeing his arm come out, aimed and shot back close enough that he only got one more off before he had to duck. It whizzed over her head.

"This is beginning to piss me off!" she yelled. She landed and rolled to find that Walce was gone, already running again. She hiked the dress up again, then ripped it off to reveal black armor. "Done with that stupid dress! Ryu, ditch the suit!"

"I like the suit!"

"I said to ditch it!"

"Fine." Ryu ripped his suit off to show the same armor underneath. "Achronyx, tag the location, would you? I want to come back and get the suit." A shot from Walce blew him back, and he thudded to the ground heavily. "That was my fault. I should have paid more attention to him."

"On it!" Tabitha shot back twice, using her standard-issue pistol. She didn't want to show off the Dukes Special until she *really* had to make a point.

Walce was now hiding behind a concrete cube that seemed to hold some sort of tank.

The tank holds plain water, Achronyx reported.

"So we're good to shoot at it?" Tabitha asked.

Yes.

"Good, because I want to make a point." Tabitha took

cover behind one of the smaller tanks that littered the roof. "This isn't flammable, is it?"

No. It is sewage, however.

"Ew!" Tabitha leaned out and shot twice at Walce with her pistol and then ran for the next tank. "What about this one?"

Also sewage. All of them except the one are sewage.

"I say we wrap this up quickly!" Ryu called.

"I agree!" Tabitha called back. As Walce shot at her, one of the tanks ruptured. "Oh, my God! I'm gonna hurl! Time to make a point right the fuck now!" She pulled out the Dukes Special and directed one good shot at the concrete cube.

The entire thing exploded. Tabitha and Ryu ducked as water sprayed everywhere, chunks of concrete rained down, and there was a scream from Walce.

"I didn't kill him, did I?"

"No, he is trying to make for the edge of the building."

"This way!" Tabitha called to Ryu, and they ran for the edge of the building.

Walce must have had some version of their harness because he had foregone climbing and gone straight down. Tabitha and Ryu did the same, but the area between the two buildings was narrow, and it took them some time to get to the ground.

Walce, meanwhile, picked himself up and ran for the busy street at the end of the alley.

"This fucker needs to learn when he's beaten," Tabitha groused as she went after him. "He isn't going to win."

"No, but he's giving us a hell of a chase." Ryu rubbed his shoulder as he ran. "He got me good with that shot."

"Too bad we can't get him back. Something about 'Justice' and 'due process.'" Tabitha rolled her eyes as they came out into the street. "I have finally figured out how Bethany Anne totally fucked me over. She gets to kill people left and right when she gets upset just a little bit, and she gives me a job with paperwork."

People were staring and pointing, and she made sure to sway her hips a little as she ran. "That's right, people!" she called. "Bet you guys have never seen a sweet set of curves like this before! This is a hundred percent Earth, baby!"

"They don't speak English," Ryu reminded her.

Ahead of them, Walce was screaming something in the native language. The crowd parted for him, then closed up for Tabitha and Ryu.

"What is he yelling?"

He is saying that outsiders are following him. The people here believe that outsiders are not to be trusted. They are protecting him.

He steals from people like them!

For their benefit. Also, he is part of the ruling class.

Remind me to re-send the memo about caste systems to Karkat, Achronyx!

Yes, Ranger Tabitha.

They followed Walce up the street, fighting their way through the crowds, until Tabitha finally said, "You know what? Screw this."

She dodged sideways before anyone in the crowd could block her and ran up the side of a nearby building, going up in an arc to come around the group. When she came down people were ready to close in on her, but she drew her Dukes Special.

You didn't have to know *exactly* what it was to see that it was a huge fucking gun, and people scattered.

They didn't have to know she wasn't going to shoot civilians, after all.

Ahead of her, Walce gave a scream when he saw how close they had gotten. He made for the far corner of the street, where several food trucks were clustered. He hurdled the first cart, spilling melons everywhere, and disappeared.

"Achronyx, where did he go?" Tabitha held the gun up as she ran through the crowd.

You will not like this, Ranger Tabitha. He appears to have gone down a manhole.

"A manhole? Why should that bother me?" Tabitha looked down at herself. "How small are the manholes here? I can fit. I keep myself trim. Ryu, on the other hand..."

"I was good enough for you to bring to the ball!" Ryu said, with a grin.

"Only because Dev wasn't available! Achronyx, see if Dev Zancred is still at the ball." Tabitha hurdled the same fruit cart and saw the manhole. "Have someone deliver a message that says I want to talk to him later. I'll just find another burlap bag and wear that back— Oh my *God*."

"What is it?" Ryu called.

"It's going into the sewers!" Tabitha wailed.

I did tell you that you would not like it.

"I didn't know that's what you meant!" Tabitha landed in a puddle. "Ew, ew, ew. Okay, this isn't so bad. It smells bad, but it isn't so bad."

The puddle abruptly got deeper as the tunnel began to slant down.

Tabitha kept pushing forward, but her bitching continued. "No, it's definitely that bad! This is the worst! Why are we here?"

"Because we're Rangers," Ryu managed, wading along next to Tabitha with his nose plugged. "And neither snow nor rain nor sleet—"

"WHAT?" Tabitha argued. "That's the US Postal Service! Neither of us is even American!"

Ahead of them, Walce could hear them yelling, and he tried not to let them hear him wading desperately through the muck. He hadn't thought they'd be able to see where he'd gone, for one thing, and he *definitely* hadn't expected them to follow him.

He realized he didn't even know where he was going. This had just been a burst of inspiration when he saw how close they were. Food carts in Karkat tended to cluster by manhole covers so they could throw their refuse directly into the sewers. He had landed in a pile of sausage ends and was probably never going to eat sausage again in his life.

He didn't even know what these two humans *wanted* with him. He had heard they were looking for him on the first night, but Kenet Aljun'ra had contacted him to say everything would be taken care of.

Apparently, you couldn't trust a Flexxent with *anything.*

He snarled as he waded through a particularly noxious part of the muck. He didn't want to think what was in this. At least he couldn't hear the humans yelling anymore.

Walce stopped.

He couldn't hear the humans yelling anymore.

He turned around—and bumped into the tall one.

"Oh, hello," Ryu said to him. The silvery coloring was still on his skin, but his eyes were now glowing red. "What a charming home you have."

Rebus Quadrant, Aboard the *Penitent Granddaughter*, Nickie's Quarters

Once she finished reading, Nickie got up to pace. She felt too much, like she would jitter out of her skin. Instead, she wound up standing in the middle of the room. She stared at the wall on the opposite side of her room as if she weren't even aware it was there. Like it was going to come to life and start speaking to her. Grim's words from before kept playing in her head.

"If you're fighting because you have to—because it needs to happen and there's no other choice—it's a very different thing than fighting because you hate your target."

Why *was* she fighting the Skaines? Sure, she hated them, but that wasn't *why* she was fighting them.

Was it?

She wasn't sure. She could think of a handful of reasons off the top of her head why the Skaines needed to be stopped, but at the same time…fighting them felt good. She couldn't pretend otherwise. Fighting the Skaines *felt good* and gave her something to take out all her stress on. It gave her a target to aim every bad thing that had ever happened to her at.

"Maybe that's the problem," she mumbled, finally flopping backward onto her bed again. She had a brief glimpse of the ceiling before she flung one arm over her face, hiding her eyes in the crook of her elbow. She curled her other hand into a fist and thumped it halfheartedly on the mattress.

There wasn't anything wrong with enjoying fighting. She wasn't going to concede that point. She liked the way her muscles burned as she was pushing herself to her limit. Few things pushed her to her limits in quite the same way as a good fight or sparring match.

But she could understand, if she put herself in the mindset of someone who didn't know anything about her situation, why it might seem a little unfortunate that she didn't just enjoy the *athletic* aspects of combat.

She enjoyed hurting her opponents, at least when they were Skaines.

She supposed she could understand why that might be a little alarming to anyone who didn't know her or her situation or what the Skaines were like.

She let the fight on Swapayama replay in her thoughts, even calling up the drone footage of it so she could get a different point of view on it. Most of the footage was simply of the Skaines as the drones plowed through them, but all three of them had captured Nickie on film at various points.

It was…unsettling.

Nickie knew she was a good fighter. And even if she

could be impatient and impulsive, she knew she was good with tactics when she put her mind to it.

In no clip of her from the drones' footage did it look like she was being tactical. It didn't look like she was thinking at *all*, truth be told. She looked more like an animal, feral and rabid, concerned only with getting her teeth into whatever she could reach next. Given the blood coating her, she couldn't even be sure if that was entirely a metaphor. She might very well have resorted to that if she'd needed to.

Furiously, she tried to rationalize the footage. It had been a drastic situation. (But not as drastic as situations she had been stuck in before.) It had been urgent. (She'd been in bigger emergencies.) It had been dangerous. (In all honesty, she had probably been in more danger getting into the mines on Themis. She was more familiar with Skaines than she was with half-destroyed mines.)

She could think of so many reasons why that level of brutality had been necessary, but she could refute every one.

For a moment, she couldn't help but think of two children on a playground, shouting over each other as they both tried to win an argument.

Finally, she dredged up her trump card; the one thing she was sure *had* to make that entire episode the right thing to do. She had needed to save those girls. She didn't know what the Skaines had been planning to do with them, but it wouldn't have been good. The girls would have been dead or wishing they were within days.

If *she* hadn't saved them, who would have? No one on Swapayama was equipped to fight much of anything. From

Meredith's initial reports, Nickie was pretty sure the girls had been abandoned by the rest of the village in pretty short order.

She had done *the right thing* by saving them.

She hadn't been fighting for those girls, though, had she?

Her voice was small as she breathed the words, "I never even thought of them."

During that whole fight, with the girls chained just a few yards away, they scarcely crossed her mind. It would have been easy for a stray laser blast to hit one of them, or even for one of her drones to get knocked off-course and clip one of them. Frankly, it was a miracle that nothing like that had happened.

Even the fact that she *had* saved them didn't cheer her up. She was just using them as an excuse to make herself feel better.

The realization hit her like a bucket of ice water in the face.

The Skaines had ransacked the village and taken hostages. Who knew what else they had been planning to do while they were there? All to lead up to another slave run. They had needed to be dealt with.

But that wasn't why Nickie had fought them. She had fought them because she was angry. With them, and with everything else.

Hate the sin but not the sinner, people said. Nickie had never given the phrase too much thought. A bit too much philosophy for her taste and she had never been one for pseudo-religious babble. Just then, though, she was pretty sure she understood what the words were supposed to mean.

She sat up in a hurry, grabbing the edge of her towel and tossing it to the floor as she got to her feet. Hastily, she got dressed, tugging her clothes on with impatient motions. She had barely finished stomping her feet into her boots by the time she was out the door and on the way to the bridge. She took each step at nearly a run, as if the realization would flee and leave her right back where she started if she didn't get to the bridge in double-time.

The bridge was empty when Nickie stepped through the doors, but that wasn't a surprise. Grim was in the kitchen, and as timid as Durq was, he still didn't like to be alone. If he wasn't asleep, he was probably in the kitchen with Grim.

She strode through the bridge with hurried steps and threw herself down in the command chair. She could have done this from anywhere, she supposed, but getting up and going to the bridge made it feel more official. Like she was actually doing something worth a good goddamn about the problem.

Meredith. I need you to look something up for me.

Of course. What do you need?

Those fuckers I promised Molly I would deal with. Any idea how we might track them down?

For a moment, Nickie was worried that Meredith would tell her it would take days or weeks to track them back down. She had sort of let them slip from her mind when something more personal had popped up. Considering that, Meredith's next words were as refreshing as a glass of icy lemonade.

I have been loosely keeping tabs on them. I thought it was for the best. I knew that eventually we would need to know where they ran off to.

Meredith, you are officially my favorite.

I will do my best to be adequately honored by such esteem.

The Skaine job database appeared at the edge of Nickie's vision, scrolling rapidly. Completed jobs and new ones alike were highlighted and pulled aside.

They have remained clustered in this area, and they have two active jobs at this moment. They are on neighboring planets. Considering that, there are a few options for where they might be laying low.

Considering "laying low" could mean any number of things for the Skaines, Nickie was relieved to see that the options that popped up on the map that had taken over the main viewing screen were all space stations rather than colonies. Skaines never played well with colonies.

Nickie eyed them shrewdly for a moment, then she nodded once.

All right. Set a course for the one that seems the most likely. We'll start from there and see where it takes us.

Rebus Quadrant, Ablapus Space Station

Ablapus Space Station was small, only barely large enough to have a residential section and a few businesses within it. Most of its income came from refueling, reloading, and long-term storage and docking. It was common to see ships coming and going at all hours, and it was a popular station for ships of any planet to dock at when they needed to restock or refuel.

Skaine ships were uncommon there, though. Nickie

suspected it was because they knew they would stand out too much on such a small station. But if they hadn't enough fuel to make it to one of the larger stations, they weren't above making that sort of compromise.

When all was said and done, the *Granddaughter* had only been docked for about fifteen minutes and Nickie had only been on the station for about ten when she spotted the ship she was searching for. What looked like the entire crew was milling around in the docking bay, and Nickie took careful note of what they were all doing as she slowly approached the ship.

The Skaines were just loading crates into the ship's cargo hold and taking inventory, nothing particularly dangerous. They hardly even looked up as Nickie approached. Maybe it was that lack of immediate violence that led to Nickie open her mouth and speak to them.

"Working hard?" she wondered, folding her arms and leaning one shoulder against the landing gear.

"Yep," one of them answered blandly, sliding her a glance before going back to the task at hand. He hefted a crate onto his shoulders and started carrying it up the gangplank.

"Anything good?" she asked when he emerged from the cargo hold to move another crate.

He shot her an irritated glance. "Not really your business, Pasty." He reached for another crate, heaving his shoulder against it as he started sliding it up the gangplank.

"I'm guessing if someone explained, like…economics and sociology and psychology to you, you people *still* wouldn't feel inclined to find new avenues of work," she observed, glancing around at the others. They had realized she was there and were muttering amongst themselves. A few of them shrugged and resumed ignoring her.

Maybe forty in all. She had faced more.

"A crew needs to earn a living," he grunted as the crate slid a few inches up the gangplank. "Can you fuck off soon? We're busy."

She couldn't say she had expected a different answer, and she supposed it didn't really matter. She had already promised she would deal with them, and she didn't intend to go back on her promise.

She bent down, and to anyone watching, it just looked as if she were adjusting one of the straps on her boot as she slipped her knife from its sheath. No one noticed it as she straightened back up.

She took her drones from her pouch, which looked like she was simply reaching into her pocket. She let them go behind her back, and they blended with the metal of the docking bay as they flew off. Rolling her shoulders, she pulled her gun from its holster seamlessly. None of the Skaines suspected a thing until Nickie started moving.

Two steps forward and a hop had her standing on the gangplank with the Skaine who had been humoring her, and her knife found his chin in short order. No one even realized what was going on until his body dropped to the floor. She lifted her gun, and she had just enough time to fire one, two, three shots before the chaos started. Three more dropped to the ground, to be hurdled as the rest of the crew charged Nickie.

Immediately, she retreated onto the ship. As she did, her holoball appeared in her hand and she gave it a swat, sending it ricocheting around the room. As its lights bounced all over the place, it worked to disguise where her shots were coming from as she shot out the lights in the cargo hold and plunged it into darkness. A grid blanketed her vision, but the Skaines didn't have the same tricks up their sleeves.

With only the holoball bobbing slowly back and forth in a corner to offer any idea where she was, a handful of Skaines converged on it. Nickie crept up behind them as they cautiously investigated.

They had just enough time to realize she was nowhere near the holoball before she fired, shooting one in the back of the head. The other four whipped around to face her and she dove away, disappearing behind a pile of flats of food stores.

She could hear them splitting up to come around both sides of the pile, but then she had enhanced hearing. She was willing to bet they couldn't hear *her* over the sounds of the rest of the crew out in the docking bay, shouting and swearing as they tried and failed to catch or destroy the drone trio.

She climbed the pile of flats, pulling herself onto the top of it, then peered down over the edge and fired once before hopping back down. As one Skaine dropped from the shot through the top of the head, her knife slipped easily into a second's throat. She heard footsteps on the other side of the pile, and she rounded it to stab a third Skaine in the back of the neck.

But the fourth one wasn't there.

Nickie looked around quickly but paused when she heard something creaking. She leapt aside as the fourth Skaine tried to tackle her from the top of the pile, tucking and rolling as the Skaine landed in a disorganized heap on the floor.

He scrambled back to his feet, gun in hand. He took aim and fired, and the laser blast ripped through the edge of the pile as Nickie ducked behind it. Her holoball, still bobbing in the corner until that moment, reappeared in her hand. She peered out from behind the pile and lobbed the holoball at the Skaine's face. He yelped and stumbled back, waving it away with hurried movements.

He didn't know it was just a toy—shiny and distracting, but harmless. Nickie couldn't decide if that was funny or just sort of sad, and she shoved the thought out of her head quickly.

She aimed and fired, only for her shot to go past the Skaine's head as he dodged around the holoball. Finally, his attention snapped back to her and he lunged, claws bared. He never got a chance to crash into her, though.

One of the drones ripped through the hull, sending shrapnel in every direction and letting a shaft of light pour in from outside. The last Skaine in the cargo hold dropped to the ground, gasping and clawing at his face and his neck as splinters of metal impaled him in half a dozen places. When Nickie shot him, it felt a bit more genuine when she told herself it was to put him out of his misery. He would have died anyway, but it wasn't *just* about killing them or letting them suffer. It was about doing a job and keeping a promise.

She turned on her heel, checked her gun and her knife, and dashed back out of the cargo hold. She could hear the drones over her head, and by the time she got back out of the ship, there were only a dozen Skaines left.

Really, her drones were one of the best purchases she had ever made.

She hopped over the side of the gangplank and ducked underneath it, dodging a few blasts. Her drones kept working, giving her time to cross to the other side of the gangplank and peer out. She lifted her gun and took aim, only to have to duck her head back behind the gangplank so she didn't get her scalp blasted off.

Gun still poking out, she fired blindly twice and heard the thump of a body hitting the floor. She peered out again and pulled the trigger, only for the gun to jam. She gave it a look like it had personally offended her, then jumped out from under the gangplank.

The last few Skaines were nearly upon her. She pistol-whipped one on the head and stabbed her knife up through his chin. Before the body collapsed, she vaulted over it, out of the way of two sets of grasping claws. When she landed, she used the momentum to aim a roundhouse kick at one of them, and his neck snapped under the impact.

As her leg came back to the ground, she kept turning. She flipped her knife to a reverse grip, using the last of her momentum to slam it through the side of the next Skaine's temple. She pulled the knife free, and the body crumpled.

Everything got quiet, and she slowed to a halt. She looked around, turning in a slow circle and letting her gaze sweep over the docking bay. After one circle, she was satisfied that the job was done.

She took a breath and sighed it out slowly. She flexed her fingers around the grip of her gun and the handle of her knife, but her knuckles hadn't bleached to the color of soggy paper. She rolled her shoulders and cracked her neck, but they hadn't tensed up like a cobra coiling to strike.

It didn't feel like it had been an execution this time. It felt...more like a business transaction, albeit a very strenuous one.

She looked down at the bodies surrounding her and wrinkled her nose, then shook her head briskly. That had not been the most tasteful of similes, admittedly.

Nickie holstered her gun and slid her knife back into its sheath, then lifted a hand. Her drones landed neatly in her palm, and as she dropped them back into her pouch, she turned to head back to her ship—only to come to an abrupt halt. She had attracted something of a crowd.

For a second, she thought she was going to have to talk herself out of trouble. After a moment, though, the man at the head of the crowd simply asked, "Does this mean we can get all of our stuff back?" He was holding a toddler with one arm, the boy's face hidden in his shoulder to spare him from seeing the carnage all around them.

No one in the crowd was looking at her like she was a mountain lion that had gotten in with the sheep.

Nickie blinked slowly. Apparently, the Skaines had raided the residential section of the station. She wasn't even surprised, but her irritation was more resigned than white hot. She supposed it was a good step.

She moved away from the gangplank, gesturing to it grandly with one hand. "Have at it. Fuck knows I don't need it. Hell, you could probably salvage the ship for some pretty good parts."

The crowd swarmed onto the ship a moment later. Nickie lingered at the bottom of the gangplank as she watched to make sure there were no Skaines lingering in the shadows, waiting to cause a scene or take hostages. The father picked up a small food crate under one arm before leaving the ship again. As he passed one of the Skaine bodies, he leaned down purely to spit on the corpse.

By that point, she was pretty certain she didn't need to worry about them reporting *her* to Security, and she was pretty sure the incident wasn't going to be reported to station security until long after all of the bodies had gone cold.

And if any Skaines were going to launch a sneak attack, they would have done it as soon as their loot started leaving their ship. She had never known them to be a particularly patient or strategic people, after all. She was comfortable that the entire crew was dead, and the residents were safe.

She watched for another minute, then started back to her ship.

Bridge, Aboard the *Penitent Granddaughter*, Rebus Quadrant

"But then again, if you let it boil for too long, it's just going to turn into glop." Grim had been talking about the finer points of soup for at least seven minutes. Durq wasn't quite sure if it was good or bad that he was actually interested. Regardless, he made notes on his holoconsole whenever Grim said something that seemed helpful.

"Like when you boil celery or carrots for too long," Grim continued, sounding like he found the very idea distasteful. "Granted, I don't know why anyone boils or steams veggies, to begin with. You get so much more out of them if you roast them, or do literally *anything* other than boiling or steaming them."

Durq nodded along dutifully until something on the outer cameras caught his attention. He glanced at it and mumbled after a moment, "Nickie's coming back."

Grim glanced at the camera feeds and cocked his head to one side as he scrutinized them. Durq wasn't sure what he was looking for, but all Grim said after a moment was, "So she is." All talk of soup and vegetables was forgotten as they waited expectantly for her enter the ship.

Maybe Grim had some idea what to expect, but Durq was at a loss. Considering what had happened the last time Nickie had taken it upon herself to get rid of an entire shipful of Skaines, he was half expecting a horror show to walk onto the bridge.

He wouldn't know until she came in, so he fidgeted with his holoconsole until the door opened, then shut the console down.

There was something different about Nickie when she walked back onto the bridge. They didn't linger at the space station for any longer than they had in the past, so it seemed like a safe bet that someone had died. Probably multiple someones. A lot of someones. It was sort of what Nickie did. Regardless, someone had died, so that wasn't what was different.

But she didn't look like someone had jammed a metal rod down her spine and pulled it too far backward. She very nearly looked relaxed, or at least as relaxed as she ever seemed to get.

Durq might have just assumed he was making things

up, but apparently Grim had noticed a difference too. He was watching her just as closely as Durq was.

Nickie slowed to a halt beside the command chair, picking up a cleaning cloth she had abandoned on one of the armrests. She propped a foot on the seat and pulled her knife from her boot, and she gave the blade a quick scrub while the blood on it was still wet enough to come off easily.

And that on its own was an oddity. Aside from the knife, there was scarcely a drop of blood on her. Compared to the trail she had tracked in last time, it was night and day.

She put the knife and the rag down, pulled her gun from its holster, and gave it a quick glance, her nose wrinkling in irritation as she did. After a moment, she handed the gun, the knife, and the sheath to Brandy. The bot dutifully accepted them, but simply sat there holding the weapons in three spindly arms.

"The gun's being a fucker," Nickie informed the bot plainly. "Take care of it for me. And clean the sheath."

The rest of Brandy's arms popped out, and it began unloading, dismantling, and cleaning the various parts of the gun. Nickie observed the bot long enough to be satisfied that it wasn't going to break anything before turning away.

Finally, she realized just how intently Grim and Durq were watching her.

"Do you guys need something, or what?" she asked slowly, as if she were expecting the words "We need to talk." "I mean, you're usually a bit weird, but this is above and beyond."

Durq sulked before he could help it, but Grim simply cleared his throat and wondered, "Everything all right? You feeling okay?"

Nickie shrugged broadly, hands at shoulder height and her palms facing the ceiling. "My gun's a fucker, but the job is done. Isn't that right, Meredith?"

"The entire crew has been dealt with, as promised," Meredith confirmed.

"Good to hear," Grim replied, still sounding bemused. He glanced down at Durq, who could only shrug in response.

Nickie spared Brandy another glance before turning toward the door again. "Set a course back to Themis, Mere. We should head back to give them the good news."

"Of course," Meredith confirmed.

Nickie nodded once and strode off the bridge.

There was a long moment of quiet before finally Durq asked, "Am I the only one who thought that was sort of weird?"

Rebus Quadrant, Aboard the *Penitent Granddaughter*, Nickie's Quarters

As convenient as sliding doors were, it was occasionally a shame that they couldn't be slammed open or closed dramatically. Nickie settled instead for throwing herself down on the bed with enough force that she bounced. She heaved a blustering sigh and tucked her arms under her head.

If nothing else, it was good to know she didn't need to do much else for the night.

Know what time it is, Mere?

Roughly half past six in the evening by the ship's clock.

That was not a literal question, for fuck's sake. I mean it's time for me to let Molly know that I did what I told her I was going to.

An empty message popped up on her HUD, the cursor blinking at her. It was seemingly expecting something from her, and her eyes narrowed as she tried to glare it into submission.

The cursor didn't seem particularly cowed, and with a sigh, Nickie got to work.

Nickie was not the best at sending meaningful messages to people. She could fill out incident reports like a champion since, as boring as they were, they could be boiled down to a template. But that was routine clinical work, and it didn't actually take any brainpower to just regurgitate a series of events. She couldn't do that for an actual message to someone.

She was well aware of this, and thus tended to avoid the task. But she wasn't just going to leave Molly in suspense, forever wondering if Nickie had done as she said she would or blown the matter off entirely. She also didn't want to just say "Job's done, there you go."

She erased the message for a second time before finally deciding it was best to avoid any sort of formality. It had never suited her particularly well.

Job's done, just like I promised. If you want proof, you can probably look up an incident at Ablapus Space Station. You owe me one now. I take payment in the form of half-decent booze. Beer and red wine are borderline. Boxed wine is right out.

Stay in one piece, and don't be a stranger.

Ranger Two

Satisfied, Nickie nodded once and leaned back, giving the note one last glance before she hit Send.

She spared a moment to let the events of the afternoon play through her mind again. She wasn't sure if she felt any *different*, but no one had looked at her like she was going to turn into a honey badger. That was at least an improvement.

And really, she was pretty sure she had run through her entire capacity for self-awareness for the time being. She was making an executive decision; she could work on self-improvement again *later*. Probably after insulting Grim again, if the trend kept up.

Instead, she rolled onto her stomach, folding her arms on the bed and resting her chin on them.

Pretty sure I've still got some catching up to do in Aunt Tabitha's diary.

Meredith pulled the most recent entry up, the words filling Nickie's HUD.

City of Karkat, Flex

Ryu punched Walce in the face and sent the Torcellan staggering back in the muck. He recovered his footing, wavered, and then slipped and went under.

Tabitha pressed a hand over her mouth, pushing on her lips. "I think I'm gonna be sick."

"Yeah, alien shit smells worse than human shit." Ryu shook his head. "I would not have called that. Humans produce some *vile* stuff. Aliens are worse, apparently."

She put a hand up in his direction. "Do you mind, Ryu? I'm trying not to think about it."

Based on Torcellan lung capacity, you should probably try to find Walce, Achronyx interjected.

"Oh. Right." Ryu headed forward, kicking his legs out in front of him in large arcs. "I am *not* doing this with my hands. Where the hell did he— Oh, he was trying to make a break for it. Gotcha." He pressed his foot down on Walce's back. "Give it a second, and he'll come *right* up."

Sure enough, when he released his foot, the Torcellan came up for air with a panicked expression, brushing his face free of muck and taking a heaving breath.

"Thought you'd run away, did you?" Ryu asked.

Walce gave him a furious look. "What do you two even want with me?"

"We're here because you're violating our *Empress'* Law," Tabitha said. She crossed her arms and jutted her hip to the side. "You know, the one that says, 'be nice to each other... or else?' There's only one, and you still managed to break it."

He was wiping muck away from his eyes when he spat out. "What did I ever do to you?"

"You stole food and supplies from settlers who needed them," Tabitha told him. "They're starving. You've pulled this shit on a bunch of worlds, Empire worlds included. You don't get to do that."

Walce started laughing, then he saw that she was serious and his laugh died. "Are you serious?" He looked to Ryu, then back. "You can't be serious."

"Do I look like I'm joking?" Tabitha gestured around her. "I chased you into a *sewer* for this, man. That's going to come up at the trial."

"Trial?" Walce looked totally bewildered now.

"Lord, you people are savages. Okay, in a *civilized* society, criminals are apprehended, charged with a crime, and brought in to stand trial. They present their evidence, we present our evidence... Well, that's not how it works when we can read minds, but that's the general idea."

"You can read minds?"

"I can't, but… You know what, let's just say you're being brought back to stand trial now."

Walce looked less disturbed by that than Tabitha expected.

In reality, he was thinking furiously. They were going to haul him back to stand trial. No one he'd ever heard of bothered with things like that. He didn't know exactly what they were up to.

But now he realized that they were weak. No strong leader would put up with something like this. Strong leaders identified their enemies and had them taken out. They knew that there was only one law: those with the might rule.

And weak people could be manipulated.

"How much?" Walce asked. He gave them his most winning smile.

"I beg your pardon?" Tabitha asked him.

"I would tread carefully," Ryu told Walce.

"I'm not going to suggest anything *obvious*." Walce scoffed. He wished he wasn't covered in muck, but since they all were, he really wasn't at much of a disadvantage, here. "There won't be any large transfers your employer can trace. We do things very elegantly here on Karkat. A mansion, some encrypted accounts under a shell corporation, a few favors from BSG."

"They tried to kill us," Tabitha replied dryly. "Like kill us dead. Deader than dead, and then shot me in the back…"

"Twice," Ryu added.

"Thank you for that reminder." She retorted.

"Things change." Walce spread his hands. "I am valuable

to them. They will reward you handsomely for looking the other way and telling your employer you could not find me."

"*Oh*," Tabitha exclaimed as if she were just beginning to understand. "I see! So you're trying to give us money so we won't bring you in."

"Yes." Walce wondered if he had missed some fact about humans. They really seemed to be incredibly dense.

Then again, that would fit with all the "trial" nonsense.

Tabitha gave him a huge grin. "Let me make one thing absolutely clear," she explained. She strode over much faster than Walce would have thought possible and slammed him against the wall of the tunnel a moment later. "We're Rangers, and Rangers *can't* be bought." Her fingers squeezed around his throat. "Come on, Ryu."

With Achronyx to find them an exit from the sewers, it was very quick to haul Walce out. He complained all the way, throwing out increasingly high numbers. By the end, he had offered a full set of guards, two mansions, a share in the city's food recycling program—which Ryu nearly threw up at—and three no-questions-asked favors from Kenet.

"See, here's the thing." Tabitha panted as she hauled the struggling Torcellan onto the ship and held him down for the decontamination shower. "All you're doing is convincing me that you're very valuable to people with really shitty morals. That just makes it more necessary to bring you in." She shoved him into the brig and slammed the door. "I need eight showers. Right now. And I'm going to burn this armor."

"Seconded," Ryu agreed. "Meet you here in an hour for a drink?"

"Done."

They went to their rooms as Achronyx lifted off and set a course for the *Meredith Reynolds,* and Tabitha was still on her second shower when Achronyx came over the speakers.

"Ranger Tabitha, there is a Skaine pirate ship far off on our radar. It is somewhat out of the way, but its signature matches one that has been spotted on Karkat. Perhaps it is the friend Kenet spoke of."

"It must be my lucky day," Tabitha murmured. She hopped out of the shower and toweled off. "Chase it down, Achronyx, and tell Ryu to bring the drinks to the bridge. I'm going to have a nice caipirinha while I hunt me some Skaines."

"I thought you were from Argentina. Based on my knowledge, you don't look very Hispanic."

"European lineage," she replied. "I've got it where it counts, and you can't get that music out of my soul. As for the caipirinha, Brazil has occasionally had good ideas. Caipirinhas were one of them. I'll be right there."

QBS *Achronyx*

Tabitha called Hirotoshi as they sped toward the Skaine ship.

"Kemosabe," he greeted her with a smile from the video. "How is the mission?"

"Well, Ryu danced in a fancy suit, I messed up Karkat's internal trade systems, we wound up in a sewer, and oh yeah, we got our guy." Tabitha gave him a cocky grin. "Right now, we're just making a quick stop to chase down a Skaine ship. Do you have any information on the *Gul'rak*?"

"Let me check." Hirotoshi frowned. "I take it Achronyx has none."

"No. And I've learned my lesson. I'm asking all of you for things before just running off blindly."

"I am pleased to hear it, Kemosabe."

"She really means it, too." Ryu sipped his caipirinha with a grin. "It's how we found Walce in the sewers. Also, how we scandalized a ballroom full of Torcellans. Don't worry, that was our goal." He gave a wicked smile at Hirotoshi's look. "I upended *centuries* of tradition by freestyling during a circle dance."

Hirotoshi's look said he thought he should have been there so as not to let any of this occur.

"Achronyx suggested it," Tabitha chimed in. She was also grinning at Hirotoshi's expression. "Didn't you, Achronyx?"

"I did, Ranger Tabitha."

Hirotoshi ignored this. "The *Gul'rak* is captained by Jin'set Keltad. It's definitely a pirate ship, but it looks like it's heading for dry-dock. It may have been damaged recently. There is a record of a battle between a Torcellan cargo ship and a Skaine pirate, and they report that its guns were disabled."

"Oh, *hell*, yeah. Anything we can bring him in for?"

"Actually, yes." Hirotoshi smiled. "It appears that he has accompanied Etoy Walce on several occasions. I see Walce's ship named on incident reports."

"Shedding more light on why he wanted us killed," Ryu pointed out.

"Yes." Tabitha leaned forward in our seat. "Achronyx, are we in hailing range?"

"Yes, Ranger Tabitha."

"Good. Hail them." Tabitha waited for the signal to connect, tapping her fingers on the armrest. When the screen cleared and she saw the Skaine captain, she smiled and took a sip of her Caipirinha. "Hello, Captain Keltad. Fine day to have your guns disabled, isn't it?"

The Skaine captain hissed angrily at her, "You should turn around and leave, *Ranger*. We are not afraid of you."

"You really should be," Tabitha pointed out. "After all, I am *Ranger Two*. I am known to be one of the people Skaines *least* want to fuck with. Also, I have one of your friends on board: Etoy Walce. Perhaps the name is familiar?"

"Never heard of him," Captain Keltad grunted. Off the video feed, he was making gestures to get his ship to accelerate away from the *Achronyx*.

"We'll just see about that." Tabitha gave a command mentally. *Achronyx, pull up next to the ship. We're going to tow it in...after we knock its guns to hell with pucks and you take over its systems.*

Achronyx pulled the ship close to the *Gul'rak* and launched pucks. They struck the guns, bending turrets and snapping a few pieces off entirely.

"What are you doing?" Captain Keltad yelled.

"Telling you a joke." Tabitha took another sip of her drink. "Are you ready? It goes like this. Humans have a system where we charge people with crimes and bring them in to stand trial. We only punish them *if* they're guilty. Now, are you ready for the punchline?"

Captain Keltad was staring at her. So was Ryu.

Tabitha leaned forward. "The punchline is that it's *not a*

joke, motherfucker. And you're about to find that out." She switched off the holo and smiled at Ryu and Hirotoshi. "I was getting real pissed off with everyone laughing at that. I can't wait for them to find out what they're in for." She stretched. "Achronyx, make for home."

"Yes, Ranger Tabitha."

QBBS *Meredith Reynolds*, Rangers' Area

Tabitha was curled up in her rooms on the *Meredith Reynolds* when Hirotoshi came in with a smile.

"It is good to see you back, Kemosabe."

"Good to see you, too, Number One." She kicked off her shoes and wiggled her toes. "Come sit down and have a drink. We were just talking about the mission."

"We've decided, jointly with a unanimous vote, never to end up in an alien sewer again," Ryu informed his teammate solemnly.

"*Also,*" Tabitha added, "I've decided I'm not going to go running off with only one of you anymore. And I am going to listen to my team more while I am on the ground. You know, plan things out, listen to your suggestions—"

"Read Achronyx's reports?" Hirotoshi suggested, continuing the list.

Tabitha raised an eyebrow, "Baby steps, Number One. Baby steps."

"I work hard on those reports," Achronyx mentioned, sounding annoyed.

"I very much enjoy them," Hirotoshi told the EI.

"Yes, yes, you two go have a boring party together. Full of boringness." Tabitha waved her hand. "The rest of us are going to do fun things."

"Preparing for missions can be fun," Hirotoshi offered.

"You know, I channeled you at that ball, but remind me to stop before I ever get *that* far with things." Tabitha shuddered. "So, when are the trials?"

"Later today. Both of them are currently trying to buy off the guards." Hirotoshi snickered. "We have a bet going on whether or not they'll try it with Bethany Anne or one of the Bitches."

Tabitha shuddered again. She could only imagine the carnage that would ensue if someone suggested to Bethany Anne's face that they were going to buy her off. "We should make sure no one else is in the room when they do that."

"Already done." Hirotoshi smiled. "Imagine the carnage."

Ryu handed him a drink, and they all clinked glasses.

"To the team," Tabitha toasted. "I love you guys, even if you pulled some weird mind-meld trick and can't quite appreciate my awesomeness."

"What is this about a mind meld?" Hirotoshi inquired courteously.

"Yes," Ryu added. "You have to be out of your damned mind with that one."

Tabitha pointed at both of them, trying hard to stop the smile that was itching to show on her lips. "Stop it! Stop doing that!" She waved her finger up in the air. "A thousand push-ups for both of you!"

Hirotoshi and Ryu chuckled. "Totally worth it," Ryu stated.

Hirotoshi nodded slowly. "Agreed."

"That's better." Tabitha looked to both of them. "However, I *was* serious about those push-ups." She set her drink down and reached over, pulling the glasses out of their hands and set them down in front of her, a smile and a wink for them as she continued. "I'll drink your caipirinhas while you're at it."

Rebus Quadrant, Themis Colony

Adelaide stood at the mouth of a hallway. The blood had long since been cleaned up and a memorial had been held, but there were still some parts of the outpost that were harder to venture through than others.

"You coming?" Raynard called from halfway down the corridor. He had stopped walking to peer over his shoulder at her. Balanced in his hands were three crates of medical supplies to be carried to the infirmary's storage area. His chin rested atop the pile to keep it steady.

Adelaide gave her head a brief shake as she pulled her thoughts back to the present, and she flexed her fingers. She had a similar stack of crates in her hands, and she shifted her grip on them to ease the bottom edge from biting into her palms.

When she caught up with Raynard, he faced forward and kept walking.

Harry was standing at the desk in the infirmary when they got there, silently taking stock of the supply cabinets.

He gestured Raynard and Adelaide through to the rear-most storage closet as they stepped into the room.

Raynard groaned as he set his load down in the closet, and with a cheeky little laugh, Adelaide wondered, "Bad back, old man?" She had to sidestep to avoid his hand as he reached out to tweak a strand of her hair in retaliation.

She hip-checked him cheerfully and pantomimed trying to bite his finger. Their scuffle came to an end, though, when Harry called, "Can the two of you not defile my closet?" in a bland, disinterested voice. "I just cleaned it."

Adelaide peeked from the closet to stick her tongue out and blow a raspberry at him. Harry didn't bother to look up from the datapad in his hands.

Leaning back into the closet, Adelaide set her stack of boxes down and rolled her shoulders. Her spine popped, and she clapped a hand over Raynard's mouth before he could say anything about it.

"Anything else you need us to do?" she called to Henry, yanking her hand away from Raynard when he licked her palm. She scrubbed her hand off on his shirt.

"I know you're still being cheeky in there," Harry informed her rather than answering the question. After a second, he added, "There are a couple boxes of backup files out here that need to go down to main storage. It'd be appreciated if you two handled those."

"Got it," Raynard agreed, and he stretched his arms over his head as he stepped out of the closet.

There were two boxes sitting by Harry's feet, and he sidestepped out of the way to allow them to be picked up more easily. It was a testament to how primitive some parts of the outpost still were when the hard copies were still little more than folders, clipboards, and papers piled neatly into a metal box.

Raynard picked up a box and straightened back up before turning to face Adelaide again.

"We should do something for dinner once we're done with all this," he mused, handing the box of hardcopy files to her. She took it from him without complaint, and he bent down to pick up the second box. They were lighter than the last delivery, at least.

"Sounds like a plan," she agreed pleasantly. As they left the infirmary, she called a cheerful, "Later, Harry!" over her shoulder and got a distracted grunt in reply.

They walked past Melissa on her way to the infirmary, leading a member of the cleaning crew. "Afternoon," Melissa greeted them pleasantly.

"Everything all right?" Adelaide asked, turning to walk backward for a moment. "Or did he forget he can't eat the stew again?"

"Got it in one," Melissa confirmed as she tugged him into the infirmary.

Adelaide faced forward again. She and Raynard were once again alone in the hall.

Their walk was quiet at first, except for the way their footsteps echoed in the empty hallways. The hallways always seemed empty now, though. Everyone was still getting used to it.

It didn't quite occur to them that the hallways were a little bit *too* empty to still have over eighty people wandering through them. They weren't quite used to being suspicious yet.

When they turned a corner, Adelaide slowed for a moment and watched the closet at the end of the hall like she was waiting for something to burst out of it.

She still had nightmares of walking through familiar halls with the walls covered in blood and the floor littered with body parts. Raynard hadn't let her see what had been in that closet—hadn't even told her what it was or let her take a step into the closet—but her mind had been more than happy to try to conjure up dozens of different possibilities. Maybe some of them didn't live up to the reality, but she was pretty sure a lot of them surpassed it.

She didn't tell him about her dreams, either. She was pretty sure everyone was dealing with their own demons. She knew he was. She wasn't going to foist hers off onto anyone else.

She shook her head to banish the ghosts from her thoughts and kept walking. She hadn't even paused long enough for Raynard to notice.

"We should ask Tracy, too," Adelaide decided after a moment, dragging her thoughts off the course they had been on by force of will. "He's *still* being all awkward and grumpy. I can't decide if it's making me sad or annoyed, but either way, he needs to stop it for the good of my blood pressure."

Raynard's mouth twisted as he tried ineffectually to stave off a snort of laughter, and he pressed a kiss to her cheek to distract her from it. An impressive feat, considering they were both still laden and walking.

"Isn't he *always* awkward and grumpy, though?" he wondered dryly, turning so he could face her while side-stepping down the hallway. She scowled at him in return, but there wasn't any heat behind it.

Just to make sure she didn't actually get mad, he added easily, "Sounds like a good plan to me."

They could hear people in the main hall as they got closer to it. It sounded like they were shouting, but that on its own wasn't particularly unusual. They were a rowdy bunch most days.

As they stepped back into the main hall, though, they realized that none of the raised voices were simple everyday raucousness and all thoughts of dinner fled.

People were racing out of the building toward the airfield, and everyone was talking over each other, so Adelaide and Raynard had no idea what they were saying. Their panic was clear, though, and they could hear the distant, familiar roaring of a ship's engine. Without a second thought, they let their armloads fall to the floor with a clatter and joined the crowd.

"Was there a delivery scheduled for today?"

"I didn't see anything on the schedule. Maybe it's damaged?"

"Does that look damaged to you? It doesn't look damaged to me."

Everyone knew exactly what it looked like.

A ship was descending toward the airfield, clearly Skaine in design. Nearly a third of what remained of the colonists had gathered on the airfield, and they stared up at the ship in silent dread.

It wasn't until it was nearly ready to land that they realized it was not just any ordinary Skaine ship. Adelaide latched onto Raynard's arm with both hands, looping her arms around his elbow as if to hug it. "Isn't that Nickie's ship?" she asked in a rush, adrenaline-fueled terror rapidly fading and leaving a sort of manic excitement in its wake. She bounced in place briefly, jostling Raynard.

He nodded rapidly in agreement, but before he could reply, similar observations rose from the crowd.

It didn't necessarily mean there was no need to panic, if the trend for her visits continued, but there was no danger from *her*.

Nickie's boots met the ground and she paused, blinking at the crowd. She hadn't announced herself, and Meredith had gotten them through the defense systems, so she hadn't been expecting a welcome wagon.

She lifted a hand to wave. "Hi?"

Keen cleared his throat and rubbed the back of his head with one hand. "We all got a little twitchy when an unscheduled ship turned up," he explained, somewhere between sheepish and amused.

That probably should have occurred to her or the crew, but if Keen was not going to call her a dumbass, she certainly wasn't going to encourage him to. Instead, Nickie simply laughed it off.

"Trust me, you've got nothing to worry about now," she assured them, planting her hands on her hips. "I handled the Skaines who turned up last time." She didn't mention how bloody the "handling" had been. That wasn't something they needed to know.

The colonists were quiet for a few seconds, then they all

started chattering amongst themselves until the drone of low voices seemed like it would be able to drown out even a shuttle taking off. Nickie didn't mind. She could see their faces. They had all looked so timid when she'd stepped off the ship, but with just that bit of news, each and every one of them had lit up.

Keen lifted his voice to be heard over the babble, grinning as he asked, "Will you be joining us for dinner?" He turned to look over his shoulder at the colonists. "It's been a bit too long since we had a good reason to have a party, don't you think?" he called to the crowd, looking at them expectantly.

They didn't disappoint. A cheer went up, though it was brief and restrained compared to the frenzy when Nickie had replaced their generator. Back when there had been nearly six times as many of them.

She didn't want to think about that, though.

With a grin on her face, she pointed a mock-accusing finger at Keen. "Come the fuck on," she scolded playfully. "Who do you think I am? Missing a party when there's one right in front of me?" She scoffed. "Of course I'm game."

There was another cheer from the crowd, and a few of the colonists turned to scamper back inside, presumably to get ready for the impromptu event. Nickie, however, was still missing her usual tagalongs. She wasn't about to run off to a party without them. She peered over her shoulder but couldn't see Grim or Durq, despite being positive they had been following her a moment ago.

"Just give me a minute," Nickie added quickly, then she retreated back toward the ship. She could see Grim standing in the airlock talking to Durq as the Skaine hid around the corner.

"What's the holdup?" Nickie asked as she got closer. "We've been invited to dinner and a party. If you think I'm missing that after the last few days, you can fuck right off."

Grim sighed, glancing from Durq to Nickie. "He's worried," Grim explained after a moment. "Themis hasn't exactly had the best experiences with Skaines, so he's a bit leery about what they'll do when they see him. Justifiably so."

Nickie folded her arms and cocked her head to one side. "Really? He's, like, what...four fucking feet tall. I've met children bigger than him," she pointed out. "He's not exactly scary." She made an expectant gesture with one hand, then started walking back down the ramp. "Come on!" she called over her shoulder. "It will be fine!"

She grinned when she heard Grim and Durq following her, but the expression fell away once she got a look at the colonists.

They were staring at Durq like they thought he was going to start separating heads from bodies at the drop of a hat. At some point between Nickie's last visit and this one, Keen had started carrying a gun, which was mostly hidden under his jacket. He had one hand resting on it as he watched them warily.

They really *were* afraid of him. They didn't look at him and see Durq, who hid under a console on the bridge with some frequency and had issues speaking above a mumble. They saw another Skaine. They saw one of the monsters who had killed so many of them.

Nickie broke into a jog, hurrying ahead before Durq

could get close enough for anyone to decide to do anything drastic.

Granted, a glance back assured her that wasn't likely to be a consideration. Both he and Grim had stopped, and Durq was hiding behind Grim like the Yollin was an over-sized security blanket.

Nickie turned to look at the colonists again, and Keen regarded her cautiously. She lifted her hands in a placating gesture for a second before pointing to Durq.

"That's Durq," she stated simply, letting her arm fall. "He's been with us since I got the ship." After a beat, she tacked on, "Sort of. Point is, there hasn't actually been just 'Nickie and Grim,' it's been 'Nickie, Grim, and Durq' since Day One." She planted her hands on her hips. "Understood?"

"That doesn't make any sense," Keen replied, folding his arms over his chest. It wasn't quite the response Nickie had been hoping for, but it did mean his hand was nowhere near his gun anymore.

Nickie sighed, chin dipping toward her chest for a second. "I promise it's not that weird. He's harmless. Factu-ally so." She glanced over her shoulder at him again before looking back to Keen. "It's a Skaine ship. I mean, I'm pretty sure you've all noticed that. There were a hell of a lot more Skaines on it when I first got it, including Durq."

She snorted as a thought occurred to her. "Honestly, I'm not sure how he managed to stay in one piece for as long as he did. Within less than a day of me taking over the ship, some of his higher-ups were going to fucking eat him."

Keen's expression pinched with distaste, brows drawing together as his lips pursed.

"I know, right?" Nickie scoffed. "Who resorts to canni-balism after less than twelve hours?" She shook her head once she realized she was drifting from the topic at hand and cleared her throat. "Anyway, like I said, he's completely harmless. He's a friend, and that's coming from me. I'm pretty sure you can all hazard a guess at my usual opinion of Skaines."

Slowly, Keen nodded. "All right," he agreed carefully. "If you vouch for him, then he's welcome to join us."

"I'm vouching for him too!" Grim called, his hands cupped around his mouth. "Just in case anyone happens to care about that."

"He's very fucking offended," Nickie deadpanned at his reasonable and good-natured tone, then lifted a hand and waved them both over. Grim started walking, and Durq paused for only a few seconds before scurrying after him.

For a moment no one else moved, then Adelaide broke away from the pack to close the distance between her and Durq. He ground to a halt, staring up at her nervously until she offered a hand.

"I'm Adelaide," she told him, her voice only shaking a little. "It's nice to meet you."

Durq stared at her hand slightly skeptically for a moment, then reached out to shake it. His grip was as timid as everything else he did, but maybe that was for the best. Adelaide seemed to find it sort of endearing, finally cracking a smile.

"Come on." Grinning, she clapped him on the shoulder and started to lead him toward the rest of the colonists. "I can introduce you to everyone before dinner."

Durq followed her hesitantly, glancing over his

shoulder briefly to make sure Grim was still there. Only once he was sure that Grim was following a few feet behind did he actually pick up the pace.

Nickie hung back for a moment while Adelaide led Durq through the crowd and everyone began to trickle back inside. It was impossible to deny that Durq was a Skaine, but he was harmless. Maybe there were others like him somewhere, assuming they hadn't been eaten. Maybe not *every* Skaine was a monster.

Just most of them.

"You coming or what?" Grim called, standing outside the door to the main hall. "People with super-speed shouldn't be falling behind."

With a brief snort of laughter, Nickie took off at a jog to catch up.

FINIS

AUTHOR NOTES - ELL LEIGH CLARKE
WRITTEN AUGUST 12, 2018

Thank you!

Massive thanks as always go out to MA. As you may have seen on the video snippet on fb, the banter really has continued. And although we seem to have left the age-old debate of meat or no meat on pizza, he's found a constant stream of other things to give me grief about – including the cover art!

Huge thank yous also go to Steve "Zen Master" Campbell and the JIT team who work tirelessly to make sure that all slips are caught, corrected, and the files are uploaded on time.

Thank you so much folks. I truly appreciate all your efforts. :)

Reviewers

Massive thanks also goes out to our hoard of Amazon reviewers. It's because of you that we get to do this full-time. Without your five-star reviews and thoughtful words on Amazon, we simply wouldn't have enough folks reading these space shenanigans to be able to write full time.

You are the reason these stories exist, and I'm thrilled you're enjoying the adventures of Tabitha and Nickie!

Readers and FB page supporters

Last, and certainly by no means least, I'd like to thank you for reading this book...and all the others. Your enthusiasm for the world and the characters is heart-warming. Your words of encouragement and demands for the next episode are what keep us at the keyboard writing hour after hour.

Thank you for being here, for reading, for reviewing, and for always brightening my day with your words of support on the fb page. You rock, and without you, there really would be no reason to write these stories.

Special Thank You to Our Patreon Supporters

I'd also like to add in a special thank you to our new Patreon supporters. If you caught the P.S. in my last notes, you will have seen a link to join up as a patron.

Massive thanks going out to all who joined. No matter what level you joined at, it's great to have you onboard! I love seeing you over there.

And for the uninitiated...

What is Patreon?

It's a platform that allows creators (authors, etc.) to share their works, kind of like a membership site. Here you can see exclusive content, pictures, blurbs, videos...everything. All in one place.

What do you get?

Well, that depends on the level you'd like to activate (anything from $2 upwards), but everything is on the table: from exclusive behind-the-scenes photos, *Author Shenanigans* videos, and the exclusive directors' cut of my author notes... (Including the *baaaaaad* and juicy stuff MA doesn't let me publish!)

[Edit: WTH? You are going to place shit in here just so I delete the crap... I'm just Patreon...something. There is a really GREAT word that needs to go here, but I'm not thinking of it at the moment. I'll leave it to someone who uses words for a living.]

[Ellie edit: nooooo. I don't understand what you said, but to clarify, it's gonna include the stuff that you say not to publish in the Author Notes! hahahhaa]

And that's just the surface-level stuff.

What you may have already realized as you've gotten to know me is what you see in the books is just a tiny fraction of what goes on in the Ellie'verse.

There's a lot of thought and consideration that goes on with bigger-picture stuff in order to apply the social commentary that gets slipped (like a micky!) in with your action-packed drama-filled scifi. **And this is what I love to share with folks who are interested in thinking beyond the boundaries of their normal experience.**

Plus, all the usual behind-the-scenes stuff you'd expect from a VIP experience. This includes more personal posts than on fb, as well as exclusive videos, Author Shenanigans, and even live Q&A with yours truly. You can even have characters named after you!

If you wanna check out what all the fuss is about, have a gander here:

She means "Yes please"

You've heard me mention Sven, our friendly local barista. (He appeared on my first fb live, in fact.) He's English, with a London accent, and Danish ancestry, but he's been Americanized. For the most part. He's been here much long than I have and is married to an American, so he's far more integrated with the social nuances.

The other week, Amy and I were in the coffee shop. I ordered up some refills and Sven looked over at Amy, who was sitting at the bar just around the corner from the till where I was talking to him. He asked Amy if she wanted a refill of her iced coffee.

She said, "sure."

There was a pause as he was moving around the kitchen area and grabbing the stuff from fridges under the counters and I felt compelled to translate it for him.

"She means yes please," I told him.

He laughed, and this led into another huge conversation about the differences in how we talk to each other. Honestly, to us (English folks) it sounds a little rude and a tad demanding just to say "sure." I mean, if someone offers you something, it's only proper to acknowledge the kindness and say please, no?

Saying "sure" makes it sound like you're doing the other person a favour by accepting it! Well, to our ears anyway.

Sigh.

Anyway – we laughed about it for ages… and even weeks later, now and again she'll respond to these kind of questions in her best English accent and say, "Yes, please".

(It *can* be taught! Even if it's only ironically…)
[EDIT: NO, AMY, DON'T GIVE UP THE FIGHT!]
[Ellie Edit: (eyeroll)]

Hot World Problems

Recently I was on a call with MA. We'd been talking for some time, and I'd been drinking something with ice in it. It's kinda hot at this time of year, and being in Texas that means the effects are multiplied a hundredfold.

Anyway, as you know when you have cold drinks in hot climates, the condensation cools on the glass and makes sopping wet puddles everywhere you put your drink. I realized that I had another puddle by my laptop and got up to grab a cloth to dry it off.

I muttered something by way of explanation as to why I was leaving the screen. "This isn't a problem in countries where you don't need ice in everything."

MA shot back immediately, "You're so dramatic!"

I'm seeing a theme here.

(You may recall last book I told you about how Amy has me profiled as a four on the enneagram profiling system, which primarily means she gets to point out how dramatic I am in even the smallest comment.

It appears MA is catching on.)

[EDIT: GO AMY!]

[Ellie Edit: (double eyeroll) Clearly I can't let you two in the same room together now.]

Steve Is Taking Over My Author Notes!

Zen Steve is the guy who looks after the massive task of getting our words published. We basically complete the manuscript as far as we can and throw it over the fence to him. At this point he wrangles our awesome team of JITers, implements the changes, and then uploads the formatted file to the Zon.

What follows is an excerpt from a recent conversation about the length of our author notes... And why we have to cut them down:

steve [1:00 PM]
Apparently, there's a deadline of today to have back matter under 10%. Republishing a batch of books today.

ellleighclarke [1:02 PM]
ah I see. Yeah, i only heard about that this week! So much for 10k word long author notes, eh?

steve [1:03 PM]
Yeah - One of yours with MA was 25% back matter

ellleighclarke [1:05 PM]
oh heck! :-o (Sorry!)

steve [1:06 PM]
I edited your author notes to: "Thanks for buying the book. Please buy the next one too."

ellleighclarke [1:07 PM]
hahahhahahahaha!
You're so funny...

I'm putting that in the author notes of the next book...

steve [1:08 PM]
LOL - Classic

I don't think that needs any additional explanation ;)

Skydiving Relationships

Last week Amy came over to mine for one of our work dates. You may have seen pictures on fb and Patreon of us hanging in our favourite café near my place... pretending to work. (I do get some stuff done, but we do chinwag a bit too. It's good to have author friends. This writing lark can be quite isolating otherwise.)

Anyway, after a full afternoon of cranking words onto the page we headed back to my place to eat. Amy mentioned she'd never seen *Dirty Dancing*. I've no idea how anyone can get through their life and get to our age, and not have seen it. However, she assured me she hadn't so we set up the projector and settled in to watch it on Prime.

[EDIT: How the fuck does someone still have a projector in 2018???]

[Ellie Edit: to those of us who don't have TVs it's a novelty. Some fashions just go full circle.]

Now, the beauty of this setup rather than being at the theater, is that we can pause it and talk about it as often as we like!

And that's what happens.

Others of our friends have talked about how they'd love

to be a fly on the wall for this…and we may put something in the pipeline for it soon. But putting that aside for now, we got into a deep discussion about relationships. I was finding that I couldn't get my head around how even near the end they (Johnny and Baby) never had a conversation about what came next, after summer camp.

I mean, who would get into something like that and never think about the future?

Amy explained it to me like this: Summer flings are like skydiving. Short, intense and your probably only wanna do it once.

Ellie: So Patrick Swayze is like the skydiver of dance instructors?

Amy: Yes.

For the record, I still don't understand it fully, so it will remain one of life's mysteries as to why anyone would just want to have this short relationship with Swazey and then move on for no good reason.

Sigh.

Maybe it's the overly romantic in me.

Self-Revelation

I had an extraordinary self-revelation the other week when we were thinking about whether to eat at the movie theatre or not. I realized I didn't really want to and then found myself having to explain why…

Turns out, I can't eat in the dark!

I've managed to get to (cough cough) [EDIT: 42 BWAHA-hahahaha] years old, and only just realized it. In my defense, this is only a problem when you have cinemas that bring you food during your movie and not something I've really encountered before. And yes, I realize this is very much a first-world problem…but bear with me. Despite this, I've come up with an excellent (and yummy!) solution for all moviegoers.

[Ellie edit: I am NOT 42!! Asshole… ;)]

Enter the mighty milkshake!

Delicious, and potentially boozy [EDIT: HAHAHAHA-HA], this is the answer to when the dark and food intersect. No more distractions from what is going on in front of you. No more worrying about dropping food down your front when preoccupied with the screen. In fact, the straw-action is probably the safest clothes-protecting mechanism ever invented. (And yes, I fully support the new ones that are made from recyclable, decomposable material. It's definitely the way to go).

And in case you're interested, the Alamo recently had a very special milkshake on its *Jurassic World* menu. (You may wanna stop reading if you're prone to cravings.) Get this: it was called Big Blue, after the main hero dinosaur in *Jurassic World*. I didn't know that the first time I ordered it, though. It was only when they mentioned the dino in the film that Amy and I gasped in delight… probably much to the amusement of those silent movie-watchers around us.

The Big Blue was made of Blueberry cheesecake. That's right – (fake) blueberries, and cheesecake lumps. AND rum.

The. Best.

So as long as you can find the straw with your mouth – eating in the dark isn't an issue!

This is my contribution to humanity: how to 'eat' at the movies. ;)

Ok, I've rambled enough and need to leave room for MA's notes. If you'd like to see more though, feel free to check out my Patreon account here: <u>www.patreon.com/ellleighclarke</u>

E x

AUTHOR NOTES - MICHAEL ANDERLE
WRITTEN AUGUST 12, 2018

THANK YOU for going through our book(s) and reading our *Author Notes* here at the end.

So, we have a limit on how much space we have, and my esteemed collaborator just ate the shit out of it.

No, seriously.

[Ellie Edit: You have at least 600 words more you could write. Besides, I'm doing you a favor. You're always on about how much work you have to do!]

On a different subject, summers have been a real challenge ever since I started writing books (this is my third summer) and it is problematic to keep the publishing effort going as collaborators, friends, and family take vacations and go do things. Generally our minds become mush.

[Ellie edit: I didn't. I've been here working my fingers to the bone the entire time.]

[Michael edit post Ellie edit: Then how do you explain all of the times you blocked out to go out with Amy to the movies and parties / poker / stuff? Or the times you tell me 'I can't do Sunday, I'll be recuperating from Saturday night?]

As we come to the end of August and beginning of September, kids start going back to school and within a couple of weeks, life gets back to a routine. THEN the days become ever shorter and work seems like the right thing to do.

Except for my collaborator.

If you haven't followed our conversations in The Ascension Myth books (if not, check them out! First book is here: My Book (that's U.S. - same link w/ different amazon website for others.))

Anyway, if you followed some of our conversations, you would realize that Ellie was in Los Angeles for much of that series, and has only moved to Texas (somewhat) recently. Then, somehow, she got into a poker tournament setup weekly on Wednesday nights (and studied the shit out of it) and now is God only knows partying like a rock star with Amy and other friends weekly.

A bit of different from LA.

[Ellie edit: yes, things are definitely looking up.]

It has gotten so bad that (I am a witness) Ellie got a *master* in her life as well. I tried to warn her, but she ignored my friendly warnings and accepting a master-slave relationship openly into her life.

She even was HAPPY with the whole situation. I shake my head in confusion that someone so intelligent, so logical, and forward-thinking succumbed.

You will have to read the next book (and the next *Author Notes*) to see how this progresses, and if anyone in that relationship gets a collar.

[Ellie edit: I'm sure he *deliberately* made this sound like a BDSM thing...now that he's getting more comfortable with writing raunchy stuff. However, you may be disappointed to know that he's just talking about me having a special house guest: I'm cat-sitting for a friend!]

[Michael edit post Ellie Edit: I bet we just lost a few hundred extra sales there... Damn!]

Until next time ;-)

Ad Aeternitatem,

Michael

BOOKS WRITTEN BY ELL LEIGH CLARKE

The Ascension Myth
* With Michael Anderle *

Awakened (01)

Activated (02)

Called (03)

Sanctioned (04)

Rebirth (05)

Retribution (06)

Cloaked (07)

Bourne (08)

Committed (09)

Subversion (10)

Invasion (11)

Ascension (12)

Confessions of a Space Anthropologist
* With Michael Anderle *

Giles Kurns: Rogue Operator (01)

Giles Kurns: Rogue Instigator (02)

The Second Dark Ages

with Michael Anderle

Darkest Before The Dawn (03)

Dawn Arrives (04)

Deuces Wild

with Michael Anderle

Beyond The Frontiers (01)

Rampage (02)

CONNECT WITH THE AUTHORS

Ell Leigh Clarke Social Links

Join Ellie's Email List here
http://ellleighclarke.com/

Facebook
http://www.facebook.com/ellleighclarke/

Website
http://ellleighclarke.com/

Michael Anderle Social Links

Join the email list here:

http://kurtherianbooks.com/email-list/

Join the Facebook Group Here:

**https://www.
facebook.com/TheKurtherianGambitBooks/**